LET'S
MAKE
A BETTER
WORLD

LET'S MAKE A BETTER WORLD

Stories and Songs by Jane Sapp

Jane Sapp
with Cynthia Cohen

Design by Wen-ti Tsen

Brandeis University Press
Waltham, Massachusetts

Brandeis University Press
An imprint of University Press of New England
www.upne.com

Manufactured in the United States of America

Designed by Wen-ti Tsen
Typeset in Calluna and Calluna Sans

Photo and illustration credits
Julie Akeret: pages 4 (top), 10, 16, 17, 45, 50, 64, 68, 72, 76, 90, 98
Ellen Augarten: pages 21, 24, 120, 121
Deborah Barndt: pages 20 (bottom), 26, 38, 60, 130
Ben Hires: pages 56, 58
Mattie Jenkins: page 112
Ann Morgan: page xi
Jane Sapp: pages v, xii, xiv, 2, 3 (top & bottom), 4 (bottom), 6, 9, 13, 14, 15,
    16, 19 (top & bottom), 20 (top), 34, 80, 85, 103, 124, 125, 126, 131, 134
Greene County Democrat Archive: page 12
David Weinstein: pages 22, 42, 95, 108
Sinialee Cruz, Kyra Fleming, Mina Fleming and Noah W.: pages 86, 89

For permission to reproduce any of the material in this book,
contact Permissions, University Press of New England,
One Court Street, Suite 250, Lebanon NH 03766;
or visit www.upne.com

Paperback ISBN: 978-1-5126-0355-2

5 4 3 2 1

For my husband and my granddaughter,
Hubert and Amia Rose

CONTENTS

For recordings of the songs, interviews, and stories, as well as discussion about cultural work, please listen to the podcast at janesapp.org.

FOREWORD

When it comes to writing about Jane Sapp, I forego any claims to objectivity or scholarly reserve. I confess that I am mesmerized by the beauty, integrity, and power of Jane's work, by the history it encapsulates and the commitments it represents. Her knowledge of African American musical traditions is extensive. Her talent at the piano is virtuosic. Her capacity to connect with young people and to elicit their curiosity, their wisdom, and their creativity is profound. And her ability to create sensitive, playful, soulful, resonant works that dignify the lyrics and melodies that children share with her, in my view, approaches the miraculous.

Listening to Jane play the piano and sing is an education in the life of the soul, the life of the heart, our lives in community. Her music exemplifies the particularities of African American history and culture while simultaneously embodying universal truths that bind us to each other as human beings.

Jane's music reflects, engenders, and deepens the full range of human emotions, from weary sorrow to unrestrained joy, from pointed anger and bold resistance to prayerful affirmation. Her repertoire embraces the distinct sensibilities of the classical and popular, the earthy and the spiritual, the ancient and emergent. Both listening to Jane and working with her have certainly deepened my understanding of cultural work; these experiences have also deepened my appreciation for a life meaningfully lived—in community, in service, in struggle, and in relationship.

Jane's cultural work practice—her approach to social change—is nuanced and free of dogma. It is informed by the experiences of her childhood and the warm embrace and encouragement of her family, her teachers, and the Black church, as well as by the cruel humiliations and constraints of life in the Jim Crow South. Her sense of leadership is informed by the ring games she played in her neighborhood, in which kids took turns "showing their motions" with the support and to the delight of those in the surrounding circle. Jane believes in the power of communities to identify and solve problems, so her strategies for change involve creating spaces where people can experience themselves in community, build trust, address issues, and beautify their lives. Jane supports communities as they work to become aware of and value what they know and how they live. She believes that communities that know their history and celebrate their culture are better able to resist impositions and intrusions of all kinds; they can imagine and work toward the world that they want for themselves and their children. Whether Jane is leading a chorus, teaching a class, performing on stage, or facilitating a group, it is this belief in the power of community that animates her work.

Jane also believes in young people. Famously, she has said that it is the responsibility of adults who work with young people to search for, identify, and develop the treasures within each child. Jane's respect for young people is clear in the questions she asks and in the ways in which her musical settings dignify their words. Children experience Jane's faith in them and open up to her with their questions, insights, perspectives, and dreams. She believes that schools and communities would benefit if children were appreciated more fully as inquirers and as knowers.

The stories and songs in this songbook exemplify Jane's approach to cultural community development and to music education. Most of the songs were composed by children and Jane together; some are traditional; some are individual compositions—by Jane herself or by her dear friend, mentor, and sister cultural worker Rose Sanders. Because some pieces might resonate more strongly with people of particular ages, the pages that introduce each song provide guidance on this. Nevertheless, we have been surprised by the extent to which college students have embraced songs we thought were primarily for young children. So we recommend giving the songs a try with people of all ages.

The podcast series that accompanies this book is designed to serve two purposes. It is rarely possible to communicate the feel of music solely by notes and lyrics written on a page, so the podcast episodes allow listeners to hear performances of all the songs with scores and lyrics presented in the book. But the recorded renditions are not intended to be prescriptive! To the contrary, we hope that choruses and classes add their own verses and find their own interpretations and improvisations.

In addition, the podcast series introduces listeners to Jane Sapp's approach to cultural work and to music education. Taking the twenty-five songs in the songbook as points of departure, Jane describes how she works with young people, the questions she asks, and the ways in which she honors their perspectives and their dreams. Jane's own reflections are shared in conversation with me and are complemented by the insights of five interlocutors: her young colleague Michael Carter, a music educator and cultural worker who began working with Jane when he was in the second grade; civil rights lawyer, cultural worker, and composer Rose Sanders; feminist, antiracist, and LGBTQ activist and author Suzanne Pharr; music educator Sandra Nicolucci; and Brandeis student, poet, and cultural activist LaShawn Simmons. All five join Jane and me in exploring themes of agency and imagination; resilience; the struggle for civil rights, human rights, and freedom; the interface between Jane's approach and the conventions of music education; the power of narrative; and the building of community. A list of the seven episodes can be found at the end of the book, indicating songs that can be heard on each episode.

Jane Sapp's approach to social transformation through music echoes not only with the sounds of the Civil Rights and Black Power movements in the United States, but with international struggles. The power and versatility of music, its capacity to build empathy and solidarity, its ability to reach deeply within people and broadly

throughout societies and across barriers of many kinds, have made it indispensable to campaigns for justice, dignity, human rights and peace throughout the world.

In closing, I return to the personal. I see Jane Sapp as a national treasure. I feel extremely fortunate to have been mentored by her and to have been befriended by her and her family. I am honored to have played a role in preserving an aspect of her legacy: the songs she has written and sung with young people in communities across the country. We have presented these songs in ways that invite music educators and chorus leaders to share them, improvise on them, and be inspired by them to create songs with their own communities. Extensions of this music and of Jane's approach to cultural work and to music education are the surest ways to appreciate Jane and to honor the legacy she most generously shares with us.

When Wen-ti Tsen, our longtime colleague and friend, agreed to design the volume, we were thrilled. His work renders our values and ethical sensibilities in a visual idiom that perfectly captures the spirit of the songs and Jane's approach to cultural work. As a team, we hope that the readers and users of this songbook will find practical resources as well as inspiration for their teaching, their chorus leading, and their efforts to transform the world. Jane is looking forward to hearing all about them.

Cynthia Cohen, PhD
Brandeis University
March 2018

Jane Sapp with her husband Hubert and sons Robert and Edward.

ACKNOWLEDGMENTS

I want to acknowledge Cindy Cohen for her amazing vision and patience. Our work together is a real partnership. Creating this book is a collaboration that has fueled our friendship. And I want to thank Ann Morgan for understanding the time and space needed for Cindy to devote to this project, and for opening their New Hampshire home to Hubert and me.

I appreciate the hardworking creative team whose contributions made this book possible: David Briand, interviewer and podcast producer; Michael Carter, project coordinator; Emily Howe, who rendered the songs into accessible scores; and Jenn Largaespada, project assistant.

The International Center for Ethics, Justice, and Public Life at Brandeis University and its staff have created a welcoming and supportive space for this project. Its director, Dan Terris, has lent unfailing support to every aspect. I also appreciate the support of Brandeis donors Jules Bernstein, Amy Merrill, Naomi Sinnreich, and Elaine Reuben.

I'd especially like to thank Barbara Meyer for her support of my work with young people that led to the making of songs in this book.

I want to thank the New Tudor Foundation, Brandeis University Press, the Jubilation Foundation, and ReCAST Inc. for their generous support.

A special thank-you goes to the young people whose voices, creative thinking, and reflections are really the foundation of this book. I've learned so much from them, and I continue to be inspired by their courage and resilience.

And I thank Ben Hires and the Boston Children's Chorus, and Jerry Ulrich, director of the choruses of Georgia Tech, for introducing these songs to communities across the country.

I truly enjoyed being in conversation with Michael Carter, Sandra Nicolucci, Suzanne Pharr, Rose Sanders, and LaShawn Simmons as we created the podcast. I appreciate their insights and their enthusiasm for my work, and our short and long relationships over time.

Finally, much appreciation to my family, Kookie Green, Edward Sapp, and Robert Sapp, who have always been there, supporting me and encouraging me. Kookie and Edward have opened their hearts and made their home a welcoming space for Cindy and me, and other members of the book team.

"This is the community that raised me. Strong and determined elders."

INTRODUCTION

If You Really Want to Know Me

When I am facilitating groups, I often ask people to introduce themselves twice. In the first introduction, I ask for basic information. For their second introduction, I ask them to repeat their name followed by "but if you *really* want to know me, you need to know . . ."

So let's begin. My name is Jane Wilburn Sapp, but if you *really* want to know me, you need to know that I was raised in the deep, segregated South, rooted in the soil and nurtured by the soul of the Black community of Augusta, Georgia. These southern roots helped shape me as a musician, a cultural worker, and a fighter.

In addition to the schools I attended for formal education, I was also schooled and raised by my family and my community. It was as if there were two families that raised me: my biological family and the family of the Black community. It was like having mamas and daddies everywhere. It could be annoying at times, because you just couldn't get away with anything. On the other hand, it was comforting. I felt protected, and I never knew what it was like to grow up in a community where there were not many eyes on me.

Having these two families offered me a range of choices for knowledge and experience. We had options to learn many things: how to grow a garden, how to make a quilt, how to make an argument, how to the sing the blues, how to think about the world in different ways. There were even options for negotiating the unjust world that we lived in.

The big musical influences in my family were my mother, my older sister, and my grandmother. My mother and my sister could both play by ear and read music. My mother loved hymns and ballads and some classical music as well. She loved gospel music too, especially songs that were soft, where the harmonies were sweet, clear, and beautiful. My sister played a range of music, from gospel to the popular songs of the day. I always felt she could play anything and that if I could only play like her someday, it would be the greatest thrill of my life.

Now in her 80's, my sister, Mary Henley, continues to inspire me with her wonderfully magic touch at the piano.

My grandmother sang all the time; I could always hear her humming. She liked the old "shout" songs, the basic unaccompanied call-and-response, and the congregational songs. My grandmother liked something that had energy, passion, and life, that sounded like you had some fight in you. For her, the music had to be rock solid, saying something and going somewhere. "Sing it like you mean it," she would say.

I woke up every morning to my mother's high-pitched singing. Whatever song came to mind she would sing very loudly, loud enough to wake us up. I woke up to that sound and to the smell of bacon, grits, and biscuits.

Another influence came out of left field. My aunt worked in the home of white people. One member of that family played the piano, and when that person died, my aunt was given boxes and boxes of music: show tunes, ballads, vaudeville, Stephen Foster, Chopin, Beethoven. There were even opera arias and art songs. I loved it all. It was as if someone had opened a door, and behind that door there were all these other songs, all these other conversations, and all these other ways of looking at the world. It was like taking a tour of other lands.

In my community, music was woven into everyday activities. We sang at school. We sang in the church. We sang when we played. We sang when we struggled. We sang when we prayed. Music was a source of agency and empowerment. It certainly helped me to find my own voice and to have a say.

There were two sources of musical inspiration in my community. One was the spirituality of the church, and the other was the spirit of the community, embodied in dances, children's games, neighborhood events, house parties, work, and clubs. From all of these musical experiences, I grew in strength and voice.

If you really want to know me, you need to know that I just love music. From the time I was three, I was trying to pick out tunes on the piano. For me, making up tunes was getting the piano to speak. Sometimes when people were listening to someone playing the piano, guitar, or horn, you would hear them say, "Oh, you're talking to me now." And that is how I wanted people to feel when I played the piano. I used to feel shy and nervous about talking in a group, but I remember thinking if I could just get to the piano and sing, I could join the conversation.

The piano speaks to me. It has always spoken to me. Playing the piano makes me feel alive and powerful. When I was a kid, I wanted to play the piano and sing all the time. I started playing for the church when I was nine years old. And I really loved the sound of people singing together. By the time I was twelve, I was directing choirs in two different churches. So music was my path to learning how to work with other people, finding my voice, and developing my own style of leadership.

Not everyone thinks of the role of choir director as requiring leadership abilities, especially in a twelve-year-old. But I had to plan the music to be sung, arrange the voices, keep the group intact, and keep the preteens and teens focused on the choir (amidst all the other things that called for their attention). Leading a choir also involves managing conflicts and learning to negotiate the many (sometimes different) expectations of the minister and the congregation.

But with all that, the ultimate job of the choir director—and the singers—was to inspire, to bring a sense of hope and affirmation. And to inspire the congregation, the singers themselves have to be inspired. The choir carried a precious responsibility. We recognized that music has the power to move people and to lift their spirits. It is the unstated but understood mission of the choir director and the choir to engage with the congregation in ways that cleanse their bodies and souls, purge the week's poisonous

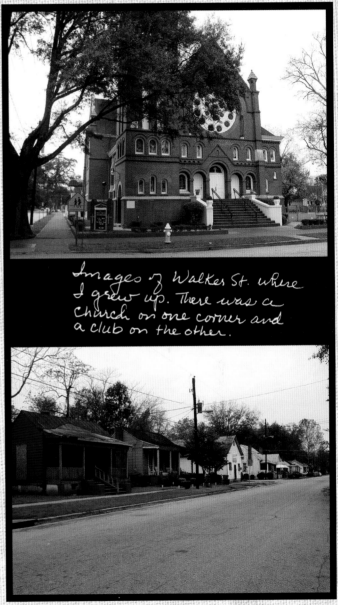

Images of Walker St. where I grew up. There was a church on one corner and a club on the other.

3

Children's choruses at the William N. DeBerry Elementary School brought joy and inspiration to all who heard them, including the janitors and cafeteria workers.

There was always something growing at my family home.

acts of dehumanization and attempts at degradation, and bring the spirit of hope and affirmation to support them as they "keep on keepin' on."

If you really want to know me, you need to know that I love to see things grow. My grandmother planted a garden every year, and I loved helping her with it. Even to this day, I think about planting the seeds, covering them with dirt. After the first rain, there would be a sprout. And with sunlight, that little sprout would keep growing and then flower. Then it became squash, or peas. It was so exciting to watch it develop. I thought it was awesome. It was the miracle of life.

And we raised chickens. I loved watching the mother hen sitting on the eggs until they hatched. Suddenly, from these eggs beneath the chicken came these chicks. And my grandmother would bring them into her bedroom, where I stayed with her. Again, to me, it looked like a miracle.

If you really want to know me, you need to know that I love to think and imagine. I couldn't wait until the day's homework and chores were done, so that I could either sit out on the porch and look at the sky and think or go into the yard and look around at the trees, flowers, chickens, and the garden. I would just wonder about life and all of the whys. I wondered how the eggs got out of the chicken. I wondered why some people had so much and others had so little. I couldn't understand why white people seemed to hate Black people. I used to wonder where God lived. I know they said in heaven, but I wondered where that was and why I couldn't see God. To me, it was as thrilling to sit and think as it was to sit at the piano and play and sing.

But hanging over all of this music and spirituality and magic of growth and love of knowledge hung a dark and ugly cloud. It was the cloud of racism, segregation, violence, and daily assaults on our dignity. And if you really want to know me, you need to understand my passion for justice, which arose in response to this dark cloud.

Where did this dark cloud come from? What did it represent? It emerged from the power of the state, from the legacy of slavery that became enshrined in laws, state institutions, economic relationships, and social restrictions. It was a world of separate and *un*equal. I remember one time I was playing with a little white girl in a lot at the back of a store. And we were honestly and innocently playing. When her mother saw us together, she went into a vitriolic rant. She looked at me like I was a something disgusting, not as some*one*, but as a *thing*. When I was growing up, hardly any interactions with white people were pleasant.

Any time we went to a store or paid a bill or went to the park, we entered that dark cloud where people saw us as subhuman. We knew that our lives were fragile and subject to the whims of the powers that be. White people did the hiring and the firing; they owned the hospitals and controlled the school boards. For the most part, doctors and lawyers were also a part of this system. And law enforcement was under their control. All of the harm inflicted on the Black community was considered legal. These were horrible days, and we still hear echoes from those days now.

A turning point came with the senseless, vicious murder of a fourteen-year-old Black boy in Mississippi, Emmett Till. His murder was provoked by a claim that he had whistled at a white woman. At his funeral his mother insisted on an open casket, resulting in raw images of what white men in Mississippi did to a fourteen-year-old boy. The nation and the world came to know about it because of the courageous decision made by Emmett's mother.

At nine years old, I saw those images in *Jet* magazine, and I remember the effect on me and on my friends. We realized that we could no longer just live within the racist world that surrounded us. We were at risk no matter what—no matter our age or gender, or class for that matter. So we might as well take racism on. It was time. And I was ready to fight.

My friends and I took every opportunity to resist. We chose not to sit at the back of the bus until the police were called, and only then would we either move or get off. In stores we no longer gave up our place in line for white people. We began to walk through the park designated "for white people only." We never got all the way through; we'd meet up with some white kids, and there'd be a fight. When

How the times have changed! Now May Park is used only by the black community. The whites moved out when the law ordered that black people could move in.

they threatened to call the police, we'd walk away, ever so slowly, diagonally, to the side of the park.

In those days insurance salesmen would come right up to our house to collect payment. They would call out to our grandparents and parents by their first names, or just call out "Boy!" But the children in my family and I insisted that the bill collectors respect our elders by referring to them as "Mr." or "Mrs." This became a monthly ritual, a stand-off. We allowed no entry for them until they said the right words. These confrontations usually ended when an adult interceded.

The willingness of my generation to be confrontational certainly worried my mother, but by the '60s, my father and grandmother were rooting for us and cheering us on from the sidelines. I didn't feel that my mother was opposed to our efforts, but she never stopped worrying.

I'll never forget the time when the full force of the racism, the hatred, and the violence that surrounded us came crashing in on my family. Some white boys out for a spin in the Black community felt that for fun they could throw eggs at the Black people they passed in their cars. My brother turned out to be one of their targets. They pelted him with raw eggs and drove away. My brother, full of rage, came running into the house and found my father's old shotgun; he wanted to retaliate against those boys. When my mother and grandmother realized what he was about to do, they tried to wrestle the gun out of his hand, and they tried to wrestle out of him what seemed like an uncontrollable rage. So they began to beat him with their fists. One tried to grab his legs; one was beating him on the back. Eventually they got the gun away from him, and they calmed him down somewhat. I was frightened because I knew if my brother had killed a white boy, that would have been the end of his life. So I watched these two women beating my brother to protect him, bringing all of the strength they could muster and all of the maternal love they could muster. I carry the memory of this scene with me to this day. I really understood something about the power of love. I felt so scared for my brother, partly for the beating he was getting, and partly for what would have happened if he hadn't gotten that beating.

So if you really want to know me, you need to know that this story is part of who I am. I learned that it takes great moral strength and great love to keep a family and a community alive, and to struggle for justice and humanity. The element of love is a powerful ingredient in the struggle for justice.

In both my family and my community, love, resistance, and resilience were always present and illuminated with creativity. In children's songs and games, there were always spaces for someone to be creative in the circle. In church, too, there was always space for people to create their own words, voices, and harmonies. I grew up in spaces where creativity was nourished.

Creativity was a way to dress up our lives. You are looking at things as they are but wondering how it could be if you added a splash of color. Wouldn't it be more fun if we could do this together? Wouldn't it be interesting? Wouldn't it be more powerful? Music and creativity were ways of imagining our lives differently, even suggesting ways of dealing with the ugliness, the ugliness of hatred and injustice.

Black people were constantly inventing a world where they could see beauty, feel alive, feel pride and dignity, where love and justice were present. It wasn't a world of escape, it was a world of creative engagement.

If you really want to know me, you would need to understand how all of these dynamics from the South shaped me in creating a path not only as a musician but as a cultural worker. I've chosen the path of creativity as a way of fighting for justice.

On a Journey: Becoming a Cultural Worker

The late '60s were exciting times. There was the Civil Rights movement, and there was the Black Power movement, which both really captured the spirit of young people. We were really pushing to take a seat at the table, whether it was offered or not. The time was exciting not only politically; there was an explosion of cultural awareness and expression as well. African Americans were looking at all they had inherited from Africa and the African diaspora. We were looking at music, history, literature, and philosophy.

New books on Black history were being published. And in the academic world, Black scholars insisted on including the study of African American history and culture. However, this was not the case at the college where I studied music and earned a bachelor's degree.

But while I was studying the music of the Western classical tradition in college, I never let go of the tradition from which I came. When I was working in the music library, I learned that they kept Black music in a section called Folk Music. So I became curious about this idea of "folk music": what did it mean, and why did they put Black music there? I came to understand it was there because it emerged from a community oral tradition rather than from an individual composer; it was created by the folk. And it definitely was considered of lesser worth than the classical music of the Western tradition.

But in terms of beauty, sophistication, and reflection of the depths of the human spirit, I never felt a difference between the Western classical tradition and the music of the Black community. So I never let go of the tradition from which I came; I always valued this music as a profound and deep part of my life. Music was never separate from the life of the community, and it was never separate from my life either. The Black Power movement helped me realize that our music and culture were also important sources of power, and I wanted to analyze the elements of that power and how it could be mobilized.

So I decided to look at my community with new eyes, not only as a participant but as an observer as well. I began to interrogate my own experience. I stepped back, and I could see all of the things that were really special. I started asking questions of my own family and community, questions about our ancestors and how they did things. I asked what stories people remembered, like stories about segregation, stories about the community's participation in and response to the Depression, stories about World War II and how that impacted our community, stories about how we took care of each other. I asked questions about many songs— the old, old songs. I asked my grandmother about songs she knew from her mother, from the time her mother had been enslaved. I wanted to know about the activities of the women keeping the family together, the food they cooked, the quilts they made, and the songs they sang. I wanted to understand the sources of their strength. What was it like to be a sharecropper? How did they survive? What were the ways that they decorated their lives to stay connected to each other and to stay strong?

There's an old song called "How I Got Over." In my work I wanted not only to understand answers to my questions but also to be a part of "how we got over."

In the summer of 1967, after I graduated, I became engaged to my childhood sweetheart, Hubert Sapp. Hubert has been a trusted partner in all of the work I've done. It was always his sense of humanity, his expanded knowledge of history, and his political acumen that informed my thinking and my practice.

In that same summer, I came across a book that affirmed my thinking about music and the community. It was *Blues People* by LeRoi Jones, later to become Amiri Baraka. Jones talked about the connection between art and life, art being a part of the life of the community, not something separate. It was

Hubert is my best friend, my confidant, my inspiration. He is always there for me. And I love him so much.

9

woven into the fabric of the community. In the book he writes about how music carried the community's stories, its history, the ever-present quest for freedom, and our resistance to oppression. I immediately saw the connection to my own community in Augusta and realized LeRoi Jones also recognized culture as vital to transformation.

While I had been at college in Kansas, away from Georgia and the Black community, I had missed my community so much. At times it felt viscerally painful. I began to think that if I felt my culture this intensely, feeling off balance without it, then there was power in it. I wanted to find out what that power was, to explore it, and to understand how the force of culture could become a resource for social justice.

And in going forward, in what I later realized was my path to becoming a cultural worker, I had many mentors along the way. Several stand out in my mind.

Getting Started as a Cultural Worker

In the summer of 1968, I was a year out of college, newly married, and teaching at Miles College in Birmingham, Alabama. The Black Power movement was in full force, and I wanted to be active in it. The question for me was, what skills could I bring to the movement? I knew music would be a part of my participation somehow. And I searched to find out how.

I attended an arts and humanities workshop that focused on African American art and culture. It brought together some of the strongest voices in African American culture at that time. Bernice Johnson Reagon led a workshop on Black music, and I was her assistant. She encouraged each of us to create a song. During that workshop I wrote my first serious song: "Lord, I Know There's Something Better." And I've been writing music ever since.

With my mother (Sarah Wilburn) and father (Elmer Charles Wilburn) – at my college graduation in 1967.

Bernice shook up that whole folklore world, kicked the door open, and said, "Here we are, Black people who are determined to investigate our culture just like you are. This field also belongs to us, not just white anthropologists and folklorists." Bernice also helped create academic platforms through her own writing and lectures and by encouraging young writers, artists, and scholars. As founder of the program in Black American culture at the Smithsonian Institution, she created spaces for Black scholars and cultural activists to have a voice in that world of cultural studies. She played a critical role in the development of a Black cultural movement that was rooted in the folk traditions of Black communities.

Bernice showed me the ways in which platforms can be created for people to learn from their cultures: festivals, oral history projects, singing groups that preserve and grow the traditions. She showed me how traditional culture is not static, it keeps growing. Creating cultural spaces became part of what I tried to do as well.

Bernice was a very powerful personality and a powerful woman. She was also strongly rooted in her community. She knew there was power in that culture. And she claimed that power in herself. And in everything she did, she wanted to demonstrate that out of that tradition come many things. It was a power that helped shape the way she carried herself, what she wore, what she theorized, what she sang. In her voice you heard the ancestors; in her voice you heard the women; in her voice you heard resistance; in her voice you heard power. Martin Luther King Jr. spoke in the voice of a Black Baptist preacher. And he changed the world. And Bernice represents that too. She spoke in the voice of Black Southern communities. Out of that culture came a woman who had a transformative impact on all of us. Bernice Reagon was definitely a mentor for me.

As I was beginning my work in Greene County, Alabama, in 1973, and reflecting on how much had been written about

Making music and building a community were one and the same for Willie King.

folk culture and traditions, it occurred to me that the people themselves were not actively engaged in documenting and preserving their own history and culture—and they were not benefitting from what outside scholars had written. I wondered what would happen if people themselves were engaged in documenting and interpreting their own history and cultural practices. So I developed an oral history project, a community-based cultural education program, and the still-thriving folk festival in Greene County.

As I did this work, Willie King, too, was definitely a mentor. A blues musician from a rural community in Alabama, he was a sharecropper and lived with his mother on a white man's property. When I met him, I was looking for someone to be in our festival in Greene County, someone who played and sang the blues indigenous to that area.

Willie King talked not just about the music of the blues, but about the capacity of the blues to make change and to move a community. At the time, he was thinking if only people understood that this music belonged to them, came from them, and was a resource to them, that it could really have an impact on strengthening community. Willie loved community; he especially loved the community where he lived, which was very rural, very poor, and predominantly Black. When he began to participate in the festival in Greene County, more people heard him, and he began to be invited to tour, including in Europe. So he earned enough money to move off the land where he was a sharecropper and was able to acquire a home for himself and his mother. In my interactions with him—as a participant in the festival, as a friend, and also as my mentor—he would always say, "Jane, stick with the people. If you stick with the people, you can't go wrong. They are the ones who know what approach they ought to take to improve their lives." I heard that from him, and always I carry his voice with me. And his example continues to inspire me.

❋ ❋ ❋

When I started the festival in Greene County, I also met Rose Sanders, an activist, civil rights lawyer, songwriter, and cultural worker. I was looking for young people to be in the festival. (It wasn't limited to Greene County, so I called it the Black Belt Folk Roots Festival.) Rose's young people were learning and performing African dances, and they were singing too, all as part of the Black Belt Arts and Cultural Center (BBACC) in Selma. I stayed in touch with Rose and the BBACC kids, and I called on them to perform on various occasions. I kept going over to Selma to their rehearsals. It was at one of those rehearsals that I first heard the song "Someone Sang for Me" (p. 98). I did an interview with Rose's mother. Our lives kept on intersecting in so many ways. I thought she was doing some of the most powerful community-based creative work, of the kind that I wanted to do in Greene County. Her approach was powerful and compelling, having such a deep and lasting impact on the Selma community. She engaged every aspect of community life in Selma, working with children, women, working people, rural people, and the incarcerated. She worked through churches and educational institutions, and she even engaged the local power structure, speaking truth to power. Along with all that, she and her mother started a preschool program as well. She energized her community through all of the forms of creative expression—theater, spoken word, dance, music, song—to tell a story. She believed that an important part of organizing would be to dramatize the lives, stories, history, and struggle of a community. She wrote plays and songs about the history of Selma. She arranged mock trials where people would litigate the Voting Rights Act and the Civil Rights movement. She'd have people debate local issues. Rose's approach to cultural work was, "Let's not just sing about the struggle for voting rights; let's mobilize people to vote!"

Rose is now the founder of two museums: the Voting Rights Museum and the Museum of Slavery and Civil Rights. She was always reminding the community of the power of their stories and the power that they had to make change. She demonstrated how to take the songs and the

Black Belt Folk Roots Festival. Reflecting and celebrating the culture of a community.

plays and move them into resistance and action. I think of Rose Sanders as a cultural force and a visionary. I'm honored that she was my mentor.

I arrived at Penn Center in Frogmore, South Carolina, situated on St. Helena's Island, in 1971. At that time, the forces of outside development were trying to impose themselves on the community and the land. But the people at Penn Center understood that the place where they lived was very special, filled with a vibrant culture and with its own traditions. They were aware of their African roots, as exemplified by the Gullah language they spoke. Even their sense of spirituality encompassed the African tradition. It was a spirituality where you felt that the world was alive, and that people were alive and connected to the world, not just through material things.

This was a community that really cared about its history and was intentional about its culture as a resource. I was there as the director of Penn Center's culture program, and in that context I was asked to help create a space where the community could share artifacts, traditional crafts, memories, photos, music, and stories. This became a museum that survives to this day.

Penn Center had begun as a school in 1863. Because of its work with the community, a spirit of self-sufficiency developed on the island. People were still making a life through fishing and farming. They were still making fishnets and baskets. They created a form of governance for themselves and took care of each other. Their spirituality was based on believing that there is some great life force, some great spirit that flows through all things. This was a community that was aware of what it had and what it could lose.

I came to think of the entire St. Helena's community and Penn Center as one of my mentors. The insights and inspiration that I gleaned from the staff and the community people there have informed the direction of my work ever since.

Years later, I designed the Highlander Center's cultural program in New Market, Tennessee. It was there I met the photographer and activist Deb Barndt. She helped me find a name for the work I'd been doing for years. She first introduced me to the terms *popular culture* and then *cultural work*. Deb, a professor at York University, was rooted in the progressive culture and the movement for social change in Central America and in Toronto. Deb's enthusiasm for Paulo Freire and the approach of popular culture was contagious. Her use of photo stories helped evolve my thinking about how music and stories could be used together in communities and in the movement for social change. She supported me by inviting me to visit communities and cultural workers in Nicaragua, and she accompanied me and documented my work in powerful photographs. She is an important part of my journey to becoming a cultural worker.

We Have Each Other: A Way Out of No Way

I came to believe that if we were going to build a sustained, energized, and effective movement, then culture had to be a very important part of it. Too often social change work focuses on what communities don't have: there aren't enough economic resources; the education system is not responsive; and racism keeps Black people from reaching their full potential. But I began to wonder what would happen if we focus on *what we do have rather* than our deficits. We have each other, our songs, our stories, our imaginations, our experiences surviving and making ugly beautiful. We know how to make a way out of no way.

And what I began to understand was that within the warehouse of what we have, we find treasures that will make us strong and help us thrive. So we have to take care of these

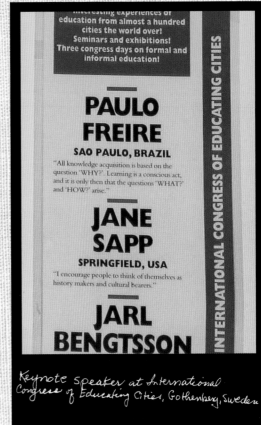

Keynote speaker at International Congress of Educating Cities, Gothenberg, Sweden.

treasures. For instance, we have to hold on to the impulse to make music. It doesn't matter the form; what matters is that people are actively engaged in making music. We must nurture the impulse and the intelligence that accompany the creative process.

We make music, we make quilts, we create rituals and songs for our children to sing. The minds that created the blues, the minds that created jazz, the minds that created dances, the minds that wrote the poetry—what's underneath all of these forms is a kind of intelligence, an imagination, an impulse toward order, toward patterns and theories of organization. These patterns reveal and embody what's important to the community and how it wants to be present in the world. For instance, the familiar call-and-response of both children's games and church songs is a pattern designed so that we can all sing together. But it is also a pattern that shapes how we can live together as a community. We need both the individual voice and the collective voice. In the collective voice we find strength and we find resilience. In the individual voice we find leadership and creativity. And these ideas, these patterns, animate our movement for social change and liberation.

We saw this in the late '60s and the '70s: the more we were learning about ourselves—the more we were focusing on our culture and what it is that makes us strong and hopeful—the more confidence we felt. I'm sure it was apparent to the world: with our afros, our dashikis, and our expanded knowledge of Black history, there was a sense that we were claiming the strength of our inheritances. This made us aware of what we were bringing to the table, and that our contribution was strong, powerful, beautiful, and rich. We were standing before the world as equal participants and contributors.

All these initiatives engaged people in creating ways to share with each other

Jane + Hubert Sapp (1969)

what they were learning about themselves and their communities. These experiences convinced me that communities are stronger when they value what they know, because when people understand the uniqueness and the fullness of what they have, they also understand what they could lose, and what is worth struggling for.

For music educators, chorus leaders, activists, and others who are reading this book, I hope that this glimpse into my journey to cultural work will assist you in reflecting on your practice and how to make use of the songs and stories you will find here. How can the processes of composing and singing songs help people (of all ages) express their creativity, celebrate their cultures, and construct vibrant, just, and healthy communities? How can the activities that surround music-making lead to important conversations, strengthen communities, and help make a better world?

Becoming Ready to Make a Better World

So why have I told you all these stories? What is their purpose?

Through all of these influences, mentors, and experiences, a picture emerged of how I might move forward in my own work. And although my life and my music are rooted in the Black community, over the past several decades I have worked with children and adults from a wide range of communities across the United States, and internationally as well. And I've kept learning as I practiced. I discovered that when I stay open, I learn something new from each person, each group, and each community I work with.

For example, during the 1980s, when I was performing with Pete Seeger at our concert together in Chicago, I told Pete I was just going to quit singing by myself. I'd always had groups and choirs, and it just didn't feel good to me to sing solo. Then Pete said, "Make your audience your choir." His words reminded me of being in church, and that music was a way to have a conversation with a lot of people, something I had experienced all those years in church but hadn't translated to the stage. Pete showed me how the stage could be a platform that created a community of voices, could transform strangers into a singing voice of one accord. The stage could become a transformative space.

These opportunities have helped me grow as a cultural worker. As a result, the following principles and guidelines have emerged in my work:

- Keep people at the center of the work.
- Remember that issues come and go, but the people remain.
- Put the focus on the community.
- Remember that each voice matters.
- Remember that nobody knows everything, but everybody knows something.
- Listen not only to what is said but to what remains unspoken as well.
- Create spaces for people to create their own art and interpret their own world.
- Keep imagination alive as a source of hope and possibility.
- An essential ingredient in the struggle for justice is love.

These principles help explain why the arts are very powerful sources of transformation. Artistic processes can be crafted to enact all of these principles, creating a sense of community while keeping people at the center of the work, affirming every voice and honoring the knowledge each person brings, listening and challenging folks to continue to imagine.

It is important to recognize that within the people before you are different cultures and different ways of carrying knowledge. Call-and-response is more than a musical form, it's a way of composing as well as a way of comprehending and living in the world. From my family, I learned that music is more powerful and authentic when it is connected to one's life. From all of my experiences, I learned the power of a people's culture. I learned how it moves, shapes, and adapts. It is at the core of a community's path to creativity, strength and power, resilience and resistance.

The stories and songs included in this book offer examples of these principles in practice.

✽ ✽ ✽

My cultural work practice has been mixed and varied, reflecting cultural and geographic diversity, engaging people of different age groups, of different ethnic and racial communities, with different musical backgrounds, awareness, and abilities. Some of the songs in this book have emerged from my work with adults and in communities. For instance, when I was working at Miles College in the late '60s, I directed a group of students who chose the name African Ensemble. I wrote the song "We Are an African People" (p. 112) for that group, in response to the cultural and political moment.

cultural Facilitator for Southern Partners Fund. (Membership meeting)

"Movin' On" (p. 80) was created with a group of young people and adults in Greene County, Alabama, in the '70s. That was a time when Black people were gaining some political strength through the electoral system. This song addressed the political zeitgeist of the community, adapting the local gospel traditions. This is an example of remaining rooted in the community's soil while responding to changes in the cultural and political environment.

In the '90s I wrote the round "We Have Come Too Far" (p. 124) in response to a request from a women's organization seeking a song to support resistance. Since then this song has been sung by activists working in movements of all kinds.

Sharing songs, listening to stories in the Vietnamese community

19

In West Africa (MALi) working with young girls and their teachers.

circa 1990's – Cultural Work (Workshop)
Place :– Toronto, CAnada

However, most of the songs in this book have arisen from my work with young people. In the late '80s and '90s, I received invitations from communities to engage with young people, helping them to open up and share what was on their minds. Some of the educators and community workers felt that it was difficult to understand young people's wants and needs, their concerns, their hopes and dreams. Adults were beginning to feel that mass commercial culture was creating a disconnect with their young people, a concern that continues into the present. People wanted me to use music to begin conversations with their youth and young adults.

My approach to working with young people grew out of something that I felt as a kid, a question that still stays with me: Why can't *I* do it too? In working with young people, I wanted to emphasize the idea that all of us have access to creativity. I wasn't trying to create great works; I was offering them a platform to say what they were thinking and feeling, what they were wondering about the world. I wanted young people to find ways to share with adults their thoughts and their strategies for improving their lives.

I used my typical approach: sing a little, talk a little, sing a little, take time to reflect. The songs emerged from our conversation. I created opportunities for all of them to contribute to each song, and to experience the power, energy, and joy of making music together.

I find that in working with singing groups, there can be a delicate balance between developing each person musically and also attending to their growth as thinking, feeling people. I'm interested in the development of individuals in both dimensions and also in offering them an experience of community. In other words, I want folks to experience the essence of the call-and-response tradition, where both individual and collective creativity are nurtured.

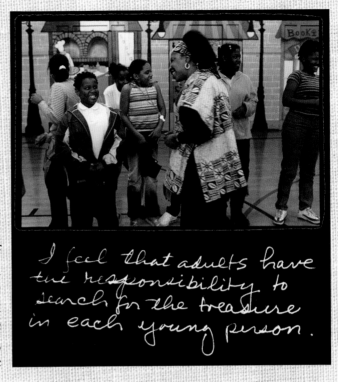

I feel that adults have the responsibility to search for the treasure in each young person.

One challenge is how to get young people's attention and trust. I think it's by shining a light on them, because everyone wants to feel that they matter. I try to elicit a sentence or a word, or ideas, or a musical phrase from each young person and incorporate all of these into the song we are composing together. This is a way of letting them know that their voices matter. The songs "Everybody Makes a Difference" (p. 42) and "One Note Won't Make Harmony" (p. 90) embody this idea in their content and also in the processes we used to create them.

As I mentioned before, I love to watch things grow. This may be part of why I love to work with young people. I vividly remember my own youth, and I remember how young people wanted to be valued, to be heard, and to be respected. I worked for a decade with Voices of Today, a chorus in Springfield, Massachusetts. I was impressed by the young people's courage and resilience. As I watched them grow, I saw how music was a lifeline, how it bound them to each other and to a vision for their future. Over the decade we worked together, they came to see how important it is to be in a community. And still today I see how young people want to be engaged as knowers, and they want to contribute their own ideas to whatever is happening around them.

I love the energy of kids. The world is still new for them. When I am with young people, I can look at the world through fresh eyes, and I find new meaning in old ideas. And I

Jane and a student at Brandeis studying Creativity, Arts and Social Transformation share their approaches.

find these new ideas challenging, especially when the old and the new come together. I've needed to let go of many things in light of what young people have taught me.

I seek to create spaces where young people feel respected, where they encounter adults who believe in the possibilities they represent, and where they experience making something together with other people, spaces where they can embrace all of who they are, and where they will not be judged.

I feel that adults have the responsibility to search for the treasure in each young person.

Children—especially children of color—love to sing. In many settings, singing is a way of speaking, a way of reaching out to others, sharing one's own thoughts and reflections. In my view, excellence in singing is not so much about how "good" your voice sounds, but about the realization that you can inspire the people who hear you. Realizing that possibility leads people to rise to the best within themselves. Excellence is also about helping people have a sense that they are connected, part of something bigger, and spiritually alive. In that space, people are aware of their own possibilities and the possibilities they have together. At that point, people are ready to see the world differently. Transformation is possible. People feel like they can move mountains. They feel like they can make a change.

It is an honor to share with the world what people of all ages have shared with me. I hope that users of this book not only share the songs but also find ways to incorporate the principles of cultural work practice in their classrooms, community choruses, and activist work.

When you touch people's souls, touch their imaginations, and touch the realm of possibilities, you will find that people are ready to make a better world.

Jane Hilburn Sapp

circa 1980's – Hubert Sapp, Rosa Parks, Jane Sapp at fundraiser for the Highlander Research and Education Center, Washington, DC.

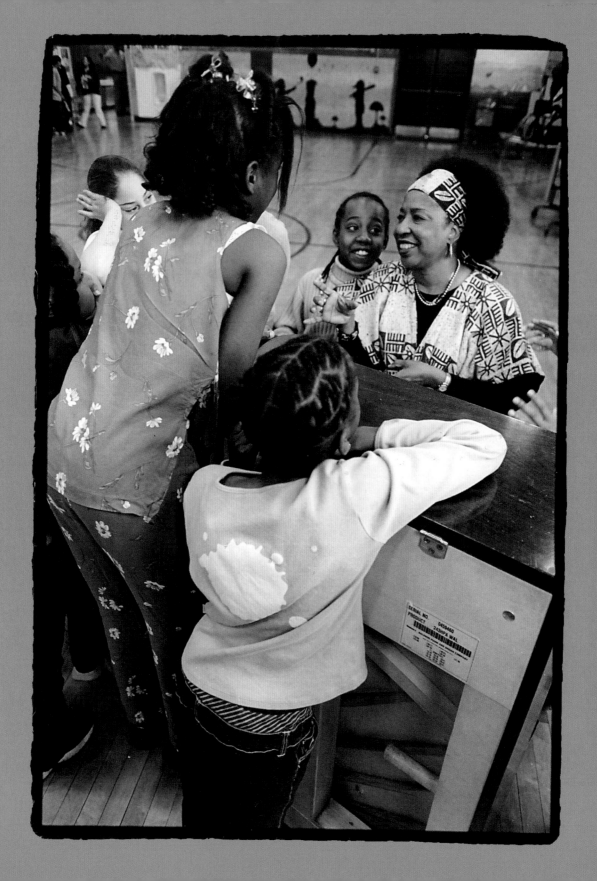

STORIES AND SONGS

AIN'T YOU GOT A RIGHT

"Ain't You Got a Right" is a reworking of a traditional spiritual that I first encountered in the late 1960s in a book of African American folk songs by John W. Work. I had taught the original to several different groups—mostly adult groups—before finding my own version of it. Sometimes you work with a song so long it becomes like a person and you learn to find the possibilities within it.

This version of the song arose from my time as director of the Springfield Community Chorus in Springfield, Massachusetts, in the early 2000s. We were scheduled to perform at an event at Western New England University, but when we showed up, we were informed that the event had been canceled due to some unforeseen circumstances. We had traveled a long way, so when we saw an empty room with a piano, I decided to stop and sing a while. We were singing "Ain't You Got a Right," and I decided to try some different musical ideas and vocal arrangements. I added a bass line and new lines for the altos and sopranos. The tenor part was reworked to make the declarative statement, "Tell my mother, you've got a right, you've got a right." Collectively, we reinvigorated a song whose message is timeless and ever more urgent: everyone deserves justice and their full human rights.

"Ain't You Got a Right" is a song that can be sung on many different occasions, by people of all ages. The hymnlike quality of this version connects the spiritual with the unrelenting desire of human beings to be free and to enjoy a life that is thriving and just.

Episode 5: *"Music and Human Rights"*

LYRICS

Call: Oh, Lord!   Response: Ain't you got a right? (2x)

All: Oh Lord, ain't you got a right?
Ain't you got a right to the tree of life?

Call: Tell my mama: Response: Ain't you got a right? (2x)

All: Tell my mama: Ain't you got a right?
Ain't you got a right to the tree of life!

Call: Tell my sister: Response: Ain't you got a right? (2x)

All: Tell my sister: Ain't you got a right?
Ain't you got a right to the tree of life?

Call: Tell my brother: Response: Ain't you got a right? (2x)

All: Tell my brother: Ain't you got a right?
Ain't you got a right to the tree of life?

Basses: Ain't you got a right (3x)
To the tree of life?

Altos: Ain't you got a right (3x)
To the tree of life?

Sopranos: You've got a right (3x)
To the tree of life!

Tenors: Tell my mother: You've got, you've got a right!
Tell my sister: You've got, you've got a right!
Tell my brother: You've got, you've got a right!
Tell the children: You've got, you've got a right!

Call: Tell my people: Response: Ain't you got a right? (2x)

All: Tell my people: Ain't you got a right? (2x)
Ain't you got a right to the tree of life?

Ain't You Got a Right

Traditional, arr. Jane Sapp

Play 4 times

Ain't you got a right,___ ain't you got a right,___ ain't you got a right___ to the tree of life?

Ain't you got a right, ain't you got a right, ain't you got a right to the tree of life?

Ain't you got a right,___ ain't you got a right,___ ain't you got a right___ to the tree of life?

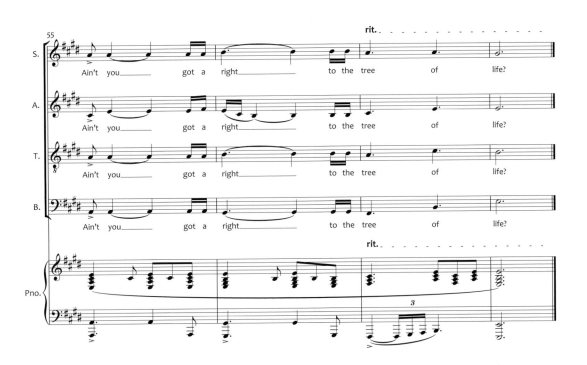

DID YOU HEAR THAT?

This song came together in workshops that had been organized to keep elementary school kids in Grand Rapids, Michigan, occupied during their winter break. I began by asking one class to describe the sounds, colors, faces, and feelings of their community. A twelve-year-old girl shared some of her words based on an experience she had of being startled in the middle of the night and puzzled by the sound—something we've all experienced. After she came up with the words, I wrote the music to accompany her lyrics.

"Did You Hear That?" is structured so the melody and lyrics of the first line of the chorus are echoed in the second line, the third line is echoed in the fourth line, and so on. This format works especially well with this song, as the response to each line makes the song come alive and gives it energy so people who are listening engage with the song. This approach can be effective in encouraging kids to listen with and to each other as they sing. This song works very well for elementary school choruses.

 Episode 4: *"Music and Education"*

LYRICS

Lead: Did you hear that?
Lead: Or was it just me?
Lead: It sounded like the wind
Lead: Going through a tree.

Refrain:
All: Did you hear that?
All: Or was it just me?
All: It sounded like the wind
All: Going through a tree.

Lead:
It sounded like someone
Going through a bush!
It sounded like a squirrel
Falling from a push!

It sounded like the monster
Hiding in my closet!
It sounded like the door
To the house of the Hobbit!

Refrain

Lead:
Or could it be my mom
Calling me?
Or maybe I'm barking
Up the wrong tree.

Was it the comet?
I really don't know!
Or maybe I'm just
Hearing things!

Refrain

Did You Hear That?

Jane Sapp
with lyrics by Molly Jones

DREAM, DREAM

"Dream, Dream" emerged from a question I asked a fourth-grade class in a school in Vermont, and it is all about what the kids dreamed of being when they grew up. They offered all sorts of ideas of how they imagined their future selves—a fireman, a dancer, a scientist—and these dreams provided the basis for the lyrics.

Kids are really drawn to this song because it engages their imaginations of what possibilities are in store for them in their lives. I usually sing the first verse so the students become familiar with the song. Then I ask the young people what their dreams are for the future. As they sing back their responses, I accompany them on the piano, and each subsequent group of young people will have its own version of the song. When working with a group, each child should say what their dream is and have a chance to sing their dream in the song.

🎙️ Podcast episode 6: *"We've All Got Stories"*

LYRICS

Refrain:
Dream, dream, I have a dream,
One that I'll share with you.
Tell me your dreams, and don't be afraid,
'Cause dreams really do come true.

I dream of being a writer.
I dream of being a scientist.
And I dream of being a dancer one day,
Yes, dreams really can come true.

Refrain

I dream of being a model.
I dream of being a chemist.
And I dream of being a singer one day,
Yes, dreams really can come true.

Refrain

I dream of being a nurse.
I dream of being a lawyer.
And I dream of being a pilot someday,
Yes. dream really can come true.

Refrain

Tell me your dreams,
and don't be afraid,
'Cause dreams really do come true.

Dream, Dream

Jane Sapp

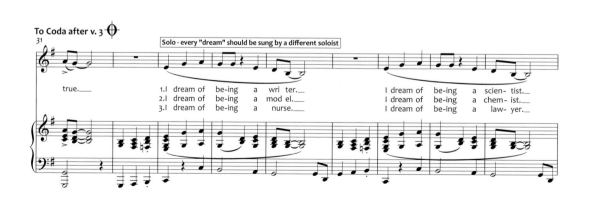

All sing

And I dream of be-ing a danc-er one day, yes, dreams real-ly can come true!___
And I dream of be-ing a sing-er one day, yes, dreams real-ly can come true!___
And I dream of be-ing a pi-lot some-day, yes, dreams real-ly can come true!___

Coda

rit. _ _ _ _ _ _ _ _ _ _

Tell me your dreams, and don't be a-fraid, 'cause

dreams real - ly do come true.___

EVERYBODY MAKES A DIFFERENCE

When I work with students in a school or in a community, my goal is not only to provide a musical experience for young people but also to create an environment in which they can open up and express themselves. I like to start by getting them talking— about their lives, about their school, about their interests. I write their responses on the blackboard as we talk and then ask the kids what words or ideas strike them in particular. Many times this leads to the beginnings of a song.

"Everybody Makes a Difference" comes from a class in Vermont that included students with special needs. It became apparent that one particular student—let's call him Bobby— had a disability that made him unable to speak. I wanted to create an environment where the whole of who he was and the contribution he was making to the class were recognized and validated. To engage this, I asked the class, "How would you feel if you came to school and you didn't see Bobby? What would you miss about him?" They said, "We'd miss his smile, laughter, and enthusiasm." I asked the same question about each student: "What if Marcus didn't come to school? What if Kathy weren't here?" I did this so the kids could see how all of them were contributing to what made this a great class. I told them that's what our song would be about, and I asked what they wanted it to sound like. One student shouted out "Boogie-woogie!" and "Everybody Makes a Difference" was born.

This song encourages young people to think about being part of a bigger community and about how everyone in the community contributes something unique that makes a difference in the lives and experiences of others. As kids sing the words, they can recognize their own capacities as well as the capacities of others, as we are all working together to build a world. This song can be the basis for conversations about differences and about validating each person's value. Some words can emerge from these conversations that can lead to other verses for the song. Young people come to understand that no one needs to dominate others in order to be recognized, and that everybody makes a difference.

 Podcast episode 4: *"Music and Education"*

LYRICS

Everybody makes a difference,
Everybody here and everywhere.
It don't matter if you never speak a word,
The light that's in your heart and soul, it will be heard.

Refrain:
So everyone, no matter who,
Listen to me, I speak the truth:
Everybody makes a difference.

Everybody makes a contribution,
Big or small or rich or poor or black or white.
If you give, you know you're gonna get some more;
Without all of us there's no solution.

Refrain

Everybody has a smile to give,
Everybody has a voice to sing,
Everybody can give lots of love and joy,
Everybody makes a difference.

Refrain

Everybody makes a difference,
Everybody here and everywhere.
It don't matter if you never speak a word,
The light that's in your heart and soul, it will be heard.

Everybody Makes a Difference

Jane Sapp

1.Eve - ry - bod - y makes a dif - fer ence,_____
2.Eve - ry - bod - y makes a con - tri bu – tion,
3.Eve - ry - bod - y has a smile to give,_____

eve - ry - bod - y here and eve - ry where._____ It don't mat - ter if you nev - er
big or small or rich or poor or black or white. If you give, you know you're gon - na
eve - ry - bod - y has a voice to sing,_____ eve - ry - bod - y can give lots of

speak a word,___ the light that's in your heart and soul, it will be heard. So
get some more;___ with-out all of us there's no so lu - tion.
love and joy,___ eve - ry-bod-y makes a dif-fer ence.___

Optional harmonies

ev-ery one no mat- ter who, lis-ten to me, I speak the truth: eve - ry-bod-y makes a dif -fer ence.

Play 3 times

eve - ry - bod - y makes a dif - fer - ence.

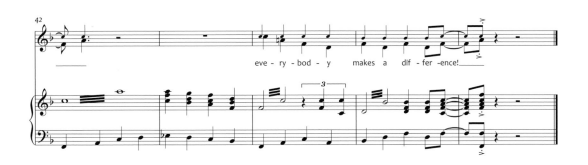

eve - ry - bod - y makes a dif - fer -ence!___

I FEEL MUSIC EVERYWHERE

This song is based on a spiritual that has the lyrics "God is not dead, He is still alive / 'Cause I feel Him in my hands / I feel Him in my feet / I feel Him all over me." I adapted this spiritual into "I Feel Music Everywhere," and the lyrics became "I feel music everywhere, / It is moving me . . . " This version originated in my work with young people at William N. DeBerry Elementary School in Springfield, Massachusetts, who immediately took to it because they could sing and move with the song at the same time. In the African American musical tradition, it is essential to feel the music, move to the music, and make the audience feel something too. If you don't do this, you might as well not be singing. The words and movement of "I Feel Music Everywhere" let young people feel the music all over their bodies, and teachers should allow them to really go with the claps, stomps, and dancing.

Whenever I perform, I try to fully engage with the music with my heart, soul, body, and mind. If I don't do that, I feel like I haven't honored my audience. In the same way, teachers and choral directors can talk to their young singers about how they should not just sing but also feel the music so they can commit to what they are doing—not only with their voices, but with their souls, bodies, and spirits.

When I taught this song at the DeBerry School, the kids came up with their own movements: "I feel music everywhere" (clapping) / "It is moving me" (moving hips from side to side and swinging arms) / "I feel it in my hands" (clapping) / "I feel it in my feet" (stomping) / "I feel it all over me" (turning around in a circle). This kind of song teaches young people how to engage with the world with full hearts, with passion, and with joy.

"I Feel Music Everywhere" is a song that works well with third, fourth, and fifth graders.

 Podcast episode 4: *"Music and Education"*

LYRICS

I feel music everywhere, it is movin' me. (3x)
'Cause I feel it in my hands,
And I feel it in my feet,
Yes, I feel it all over me.

I feel joy everywhere, it is movin' me. (3x)
'Cause I feel it in my hands.
And I feel it in my feet.
Yes, I feel it all over me.

I feel a song everywhere, it is movin' me. (3x)
'Cause I feel it in my hands.
And I feel it in my feet.
Yes, I feel it all over me.

I feel love everywhere, it is movin' me. (3x)
'Cause I feel it in my hands.
And I feel it in my feet.
Yes, I feel it all over me.

I feel music everywhere, it is movin' me. (3x)
'Cause I feel it in my hands.
And I feel it in my feet.
Yes, I feel it all over me.

I Feel Music Everywhere

Jane Sapp

1.I feel_ mu - sic eve - ry where,
2.joy_
3.song_
4.love_
5.mu - sic

it is mo-vin' me._ I feel_ mu - sic eve-ry where,_
I feel_ joy_
I feel a song_
I feel_ love_
I feel_ mu - sic

I WANT TO BE STRONG

This song was created in a workshop in Little Rock, Arkansas, and presented to a conference organized by the activist, feminist, and gay rights advocate Suzanne Pharr. Suzanne wanted the conference program to include space for the participation of young people, so she invited me to lead a group of them in a songwriting workshop. I began by asking the young people, who were mostly African American, about their lives and the issues they were facing. During the discussion, a teenager mentioned that more than anything else, she wanted to be strong. She said she wanted to be like her mother and her grandmother, who she saw as the ultimate symbols of strength. Once she said that, the discussion became about how the young people wanted to be perceived by others and what it meant to be strong, which led to the first line of the song—"I want to be strong, no matter what's going on."

The lyrics are pulled directly from what this group of young people said throughout the discussion. It became clear that they were particularly concerned with pushing against what they saw as society's low expectations for them. They knew that they had the capacity to be more than McDonald's workers. The song embodies their hope for the future and their determination to be recognized for their full potential. I think the feelings of these young people can resonate across many different communities, which is why this song lends itself to the creation of new lyrics (especially during the spoken word portion). I am always impressed by the seriousness with which young people reflect on their lives.

🎙️ Episode 1: *"Imagination and Agency"* and episode 7: *"Building Community"*

LYRICS

Refrain:
(First time, lead voice only)
I want to be strong, no matter what's going on.
I want to be somebody, I just want to sing my song.
I want to be a doctor or lawyer, something fancy like that.
Don't want to work at McDonald's for a low paycheck.

Spoken word:
I wonder where I'll be in a few years.
Will I be gone, or will I still be here?
I wonder what my future will be like.
Will I still be able to fly a kite?
Or will my sky be in sight?
I wonder if my home will be here
And if people will be near.
Or will they even give a care
With all this gangbanging and stuff.
I think I've had enough;
It's time for me to get kind of tough.
Young people are dying
And our parents are still crying.
Yeah, I know it, it's a shame
And if all the young people die,
There will be no one here to try.
And so we must survive!

Refrain (add harmony)

Spoken word:
I wonder, I worry, contrary to this,
I think it's about time parents try and stop this
And change the way we're being treated today.
So when you end up in a mix,
What do you have to say?
What we don't realize is they're tryin' to help us out.
That's the reason why they fuss and they shout.
Some of us think we could do on our own,
But let me tell y'all: you see, you're wrong!

Refrain (2x)

I want to be strong, no matter what's going on. (2x)

I Want to Be Strong

Jane Sapp

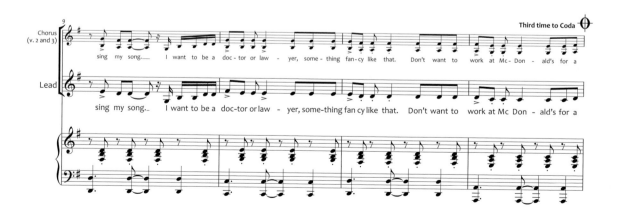

low pay - check.___ 1.I won-der where I'll be in a few years. Will I be gone, or will I still be here? I won-der what my

fu - ture will be like. Will I still be a - ble to fly a kite? Or will my sky be in sight? I won-der if my

home will be here and if peo-ple will be near. Or will they e - ven give a care, with all this gang

- bang-ing and stuff. I think I've had e-nough; it's time for me to get kind of tough. Young peo-ple are

I WANT TO KNOW

This song was written by a group of fifth graders from Mount Vernon Elementary School in Newark, New Jersey. I began the class by asking the students what tickled their curiosity about the world around them—the places, the people, the earth, and their own lives. The result of our conversation was a rhythmic song that, from a young person's point of view, sounds like a song from their favorite movie. Children love this song because it's catchy and fun. It helps them identify the things they want to know as well as what their classmates want to know. It's a song that celebrates the diversity of learning and curiosity, and it can help children awaken their sense of themselves as hungry seekers of knowledge.

When teaching this song, teachers can begin by asking their students what things they wonder about. Give them prompts like "I wonder why . . ." and "I wonder if . . . " and "I wonder who, or how, or when . . ." Also ask big picture questions like "Is there life on Mars?" When children are led into this enormous place of possibility, it opens up their imaginations, it engages them with the world and surrounds everything with a question.

As I taught this song throughout the years, lyrics by students at the North Harlem Elementary School in Augusta, Georgia, and the Boston Children's Chorus have been added. I've included five verses of this song to give examples of the kinds of ideas young people can formulate, so teachers and choral directors should feel free to use any of them and to add ideas from their own students.

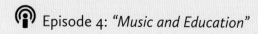 Episode 4: *"Music and Education"*

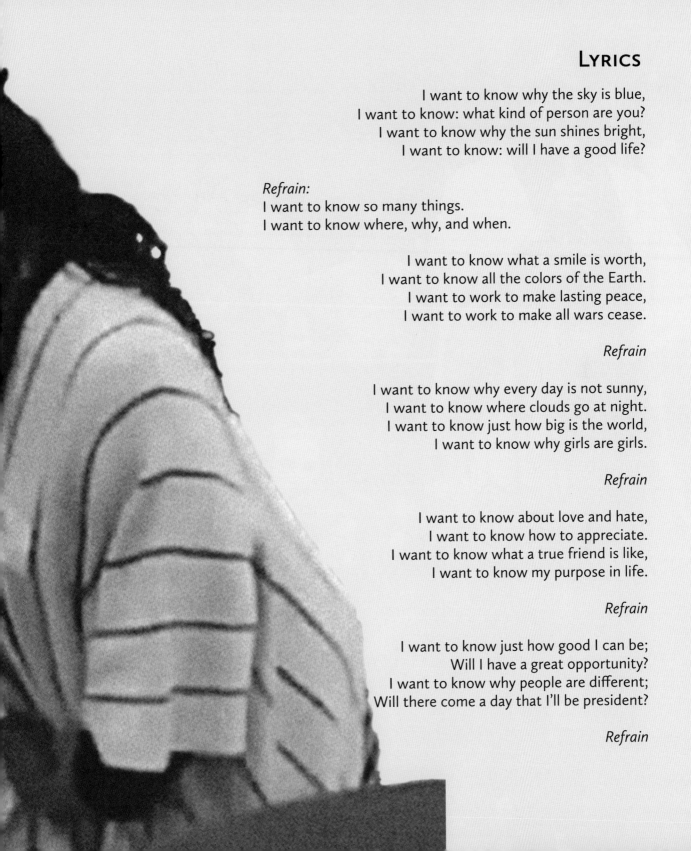

LYRICS

I want to know why the sky is blue,
I want to know: what kind of person are you?
I want to know why the sun shines bright,
I want to know: will I have a good life?

Refrain:
I want to know so many things.
I want to know where, why, and when.

I want to know what a smile is worth,
I want to know all the colors of the Earth.
I want to work to make lasting peace,
I want to work to make all wars cease.

Refrain

I want to know why every day is not sunny,
I want to know where clouds go at night.
I want to know just how big is the world,
I want to know why girls are girls.

Refrain

I want to know about love and hate,
I want to know how to appreciate.
I want to know what a true friend is like,
I want to know my purpose in life.

Refrain

I want to know just how good I can be;
Will I have a great opportunity?
I want to know why people are different;
Will there come a day that I'll be president?

Refrain

I Want to Know

Jane Sapp

Moderate

1. I want to know_why the
2. I want to know_what a
3. I want to know_why eve-ry
4. I want to know_ a - bout
5. I want to know_just how

sky__ is blue,__ I want to know:__ what kind of per-son are you?__ I want to know__ why the
smile is worth, I want to know__ all the co-lors of the Earth. I want to work__ to make
day is not sun-ny, I want to know__ where clouds go__ at night. I want to know__ just how
love_ and hate, I want to know__ how to ap - pre - ci - ate.__ I want to know__ what a
good I can be;__ Will I have a__ great op-por - tu - ni - ty? I want to know__ why peo - ple

sun__ shines bright, I want to know: will I have a good life?__ I__ want to know
last - ing peace: I want to work to make all__ wars cease.
big is the world, I want to know why girls__ are girls.
true friend is like,__ I want to know my__ pur-pose in life.
are dif - fer - ent;__ Will there come a day that I'll be pres - i - dent?

so__ ma-ny things. I__ want to know where, why, and when.

1.2. **3.** when.

59

I WANT TO LIFT MY SISTER UP

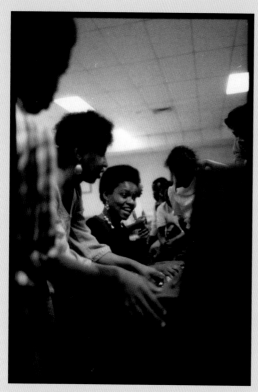

This song was written by Faya Ora Rose Touré, aka Rose Sanders, a civil rights attorney, playwright, songwriter, activist, cultural worker, and organizer in Selma, Alabama . . . and my very good friend. With her husband, Hank Sanders, an Alabama state senator, she started a law firm in Selma in 1971 and took on many civil rights cases. Rose and Hank are the founders of the annual Selma Bridge Crossing Jubilee, commemorating the march from Selma to Montgomery.

Rose wrote this song for the 21st Century Youth Leadership Movement, an organization founded in 1985 that trains youth community leaders and organizers. "I Want to Lift My Sister Up" encourages us to understand that we are all made stronger when we work together. Rose composed this song to express that for people who are working for a more just world, the journey may be long and hard, but we'll get there if we lift each other up.

The first time I heard this song, the message that stuck with me was about interdependence—"If I don't lift you up, I'll fall down." Our greatest source of resistance and resilience is in our collective strength and knowledge. Teachers and cultural workers can apply this song to so many situations. Our classes and our communities are so much stronger when we see ourselves as part of each other's lives. We sing out our solidarity with others on life's journey. When hatred exists between people, it means part of them is not whole, so no one is winning. We win when we're lifting each other up.

Episode 2: *"Resilience and Transformation,"* and episode 7: *"Building Community"*
Rose Sanders discusses her music and work in episode 3: *"Freedom and Justice"*

LYRICS

Suggested vocal arrangement: Altos take the lead and melody
I want to lift my sister up,
She is not heavy, no.
I want to lift my sister up,
She is not heavy, no, no, no.
I want to lift my sister up,
She is not heavy, no.
If I don't lift her up,
I will fall down, down, down, down, down.

I want to lift my brother up,
He is not heavy, no.
I want to lift my brother up,
He is not heavy, no, no, no.
I want to lift my brother up,
He is not heavy, no.
If I don't lift him up,
I will fall down, down, down, down, down.

I want to lift my people up,
They are not heavy, no.
I want to lift my people up,
They are not heavy, no, no, no.
I want to lift my people up,
They are not heavy, no.
If I don't lift them up,
I will fall down, down, down, down, down.

I want to lift my sister up,
She is not heavy, no.
I want to lift my sister up,
She is not heavy, no, no, no.
I want to lift my sister up,
She is not heavy, no.
If I don't lift her up (3x)
I will fall down, down, down, down, down.

I Want To Lift My Sister Up

Rose Sanders
arr. Jane Sapp

Moderate

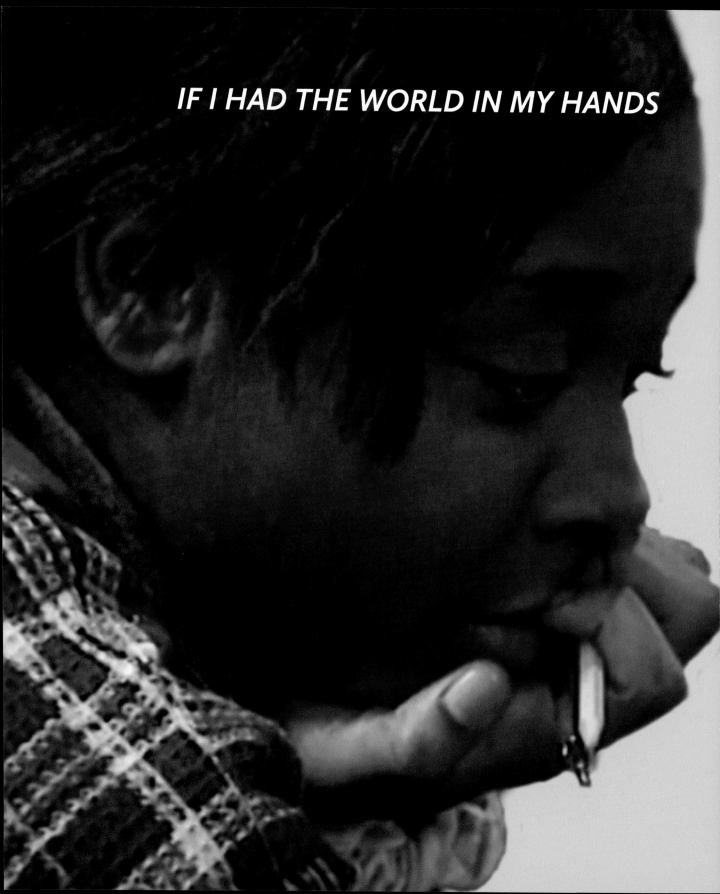

"If I Had the World in My Hands" comes from children in Grand Rapids, Michigan, during a winter break public library program in the 1990s. They were mostly children of color from a range of communities in Grand Rapids. As always, I wanted to know more about the young people before me, so I asked them questions: What are your dreams? What does your community look like? Is it a good place to be? Are you happy there? What changes would you make? These were very broad questions that helped them explore their feelings about themselves and their surroundings. Finally, the discussion led me to ask them what they would do if they had the world "in their hands."

Since then I've taught this song to many other groups—mostly middle and high schools students—and each group has been eager to add their own lyrics. What's most surprising is that no group has ever come up with lyrics about enacting vengeance or inflicting damage on any other group or individual. To the contrary, most groups seek to add lyrics about removing misery and pain from the world. I encourage teachers and cultural workers to be mindful that the lyrics of this song provide a window into what the world looks like for the young people who experience it.

 Episode 1: *"Imagination and Agency"*

LYRICS

If I had the world in my hands,
That's the day that things would start to change.
If I had the world in my hands,
Everyone could all live again.
I would take out the guns and drugs
If I had the world in my hands,
If I had the world.

If I had the world in my hands,
I would want to keep it for myself.
I'd respect it like it was my mother,
And praise God and love him,
If I had the world in my hands,
If I had the world.

If the world would listen to me,
I'd heal the sick and set all slaves free.
If the world would listen to me,
It would be a nicer place to be.
There would be no misery
If I had the world in my hands,
If I had the world,
If I had the world.

Optional repetition for emphasis:
There would be no misery
If I had the world in my hands.

If I Had the World in My Hands

Jane Sapp

Performance possibility:
Different soloist at each "solo" marking

1.If I had the world in my hands,___ that's the day that things would start to___ change.

If I had the world in my hands,___ eve-ry-one could all live a-gain.___ I would

take out the guns and drugs if I had the world___ in my hands,___ if I had the world.

2.If I had the world in my hands,___ I would want to keep it for_ my - self.___

66

IF YOU MISS ME
FROM THE BACK OF THE BUS

"If You Miss Me from the Back of the Bus" is a traditional spiritual that was adapted by Carver Neblett and became a powerful freedom song. The opening lyrics reference Rosa Parks and defiance of racial segregation on city buses in Montgomery, Alabama, in 1955. When I present this song to students, I begin by talking about my experiences growing up in the South under the segregation of the Jim Crow laws. Stories like these help kids have a personal connection to the concepts of the song and as a result, they are more engaged in learning about Rosa Parks and the Civil Rights movement. (See page 23 for a picture of Rosa Parks.)

I tell them what it was like for me as a little girl at that time in Augusta, Georgia, and how African Americans had to ride at the back of the bus in those days. When I told a group of kids that if the bus was full and I was sitting, I would have to give up my seat for a white person to sit down, they said things like, "Oh Ms. Sapp, did that really happen? Were you mad?" I told them that I wasn't happy about it, and that later a lot of people got together and decided, "We're not doing this anymore." I explained that many people were very angry about this, so we would sing "If You Miss Me from the Back of the Bus" to keep up our spirits, our courage, our energy, and our joy.

In the '90s, when I played this song for a school chorus with mostly African American kids in Springfield, Massachusetts, I asked them, "You're in the front of the bus, and then the driver's seat. What's next?" One student said, "The White House!" This was long before Barack Obama became president. I added this idea to the song, and the verse became, "In the future if you're looking for me, and you can't find me nowhere / You just come on over to the White House, and I'll be president there."

 Episode 5: *"Music and Human Rights"*

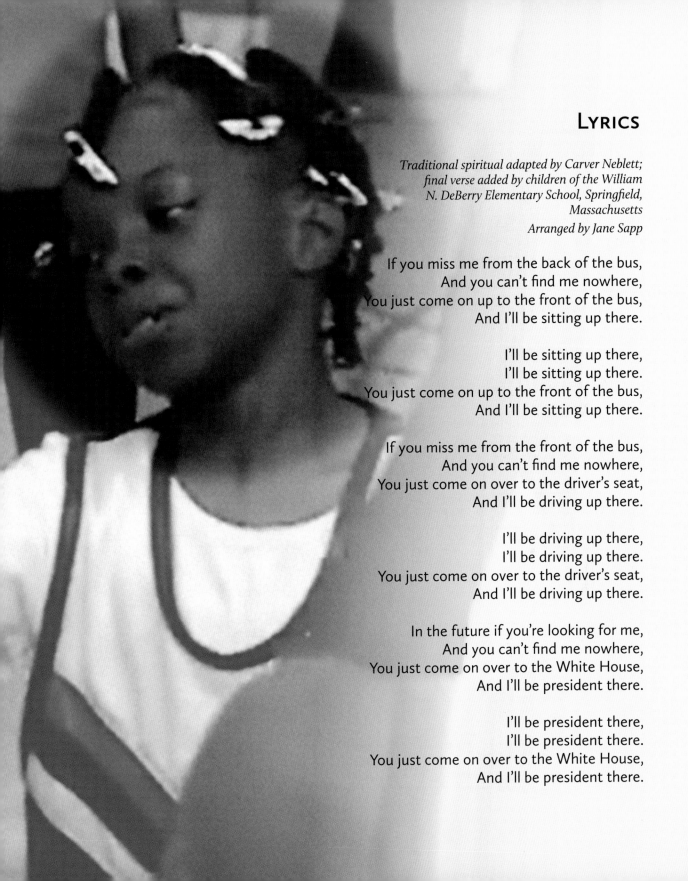

LYRICS

*Traditional spiritual adapted by Carver Neblett;
final verse added by children of the William
N. DeBerry Elementary School, Springfield,
Massachusetts*
Arranged by Jane Sapp

If you miss me from the back of the bus,
And you can't find me nowhere,
You just come on up to the front of the bus,
And I'll be sitting up there.

I'll be sitting up there,
I'll be sitting up there.
You just come on up to the front of the bus,
And I'll be sitting up there.

If you miss me from the front of the bus,
And you can't find me nowhere,
You just come on over to the driver's seat,
And I'll be driving up there.

I'll be driving up there,
I'll be driving up there.
You just come on over to the driver's seat,
And I'll be driving up there.

In the future if you're looking for me,
And you can't find me nowhere,
You just come on over to the White House,
And I'll be president there.

I'll be president there,
I'll be president there.
You just come on over to the White House,
And I'll be president there.

If You Miss Me from the Back of the Bus

Traditional spiritual adapted by Carver Neblett
arr. Jane Sapp

there.   You just   come on   up   to the front of the bus,   and
there.   You just   come on   o – ver to the dri – ver's seat,   and
there.   You just   come on   o – ver to the White____ House,   and

I'll   be sit – ting up   there.
I'll   be driv – ing up   there.
I'll   be pres – i – dent   there.

1.2.

3.

LET ME BE YOUR FRIEND

"Let Me Be Your Friend" was written in the 1990s by the father of one of the students at the William N. DeBerry Elementary School in Springfield, Massachusetts. Apostle Gregory Brown was the vice president of the school's Parent-Teacher Organization, and he would visit my chorus rehearsals from time to time. One day he sat down at the piano and started singing this song—one that he used in his own youth work to help kids open up to each other. I loved it so much I offered to teach it to the children. The root of the song is not just building community, but how we see each other: "Think of us as one, / Think of me as we. / Let me be your friend." When I sang it to the children at DeBerry, I asked them questions about what it meant for all of us to be friends. Soon they began to add their own verses: "Let's share our problems, / Together we can solve them. / Let me be your friend."

When working with young people, I think it is important to talk through the lyrics of songs with them, because it strengthens them in their own meaning-making processes. I also deliberately provided solo parts in this song so that young people with especially gifted voices have an opportunity to be heard. Solos are particularly useful for instances when there is limited time for creating harmonies. When young people sing this song, you can hear and feel the layers of what is meant by "friend."

Episode 7: *"Building Community"*

LYRICS

Solo:
Think of us one,
Think of me as we.
Let me be your friend. (2x)

Whenever you are down,
I'll be around.
Let me be your friend. (2x)

Refrain (all):
Let's walk together,
As sisters and brothers,
Let me be your friend. (2x)

Solo:
Let's share our problems,
Together we can solve them.
Let me be your friend. (2x)

Refrain (all):
Think of us as one,
Think of me as we.
Let me be your friend. (2x)

Let me be your friend.
(*Repeat ad lib*)

Let Me Be Your Friend

Music and lyrics by Gregory Brown
arr. Jane Sapp

Soloist on v. 1, 2, and 3
All sing v. 4

1.Think of us as one,____
2.When - ev - er you are down,____
3.Let's share our prob - lems,
4.Think of us as one,____

think of me as we.____
I'll be a - round.
to-geth-er we can solve____them.
think of me as we.____

Let me be____your friend.____

To Coda
on v. 4

Let me be____your friend.

Chorus

Lead

All sing

Let's walk to - geth - er, as sis - ters and bro-

Let's walk to - geth - er, as sis - ters and bro

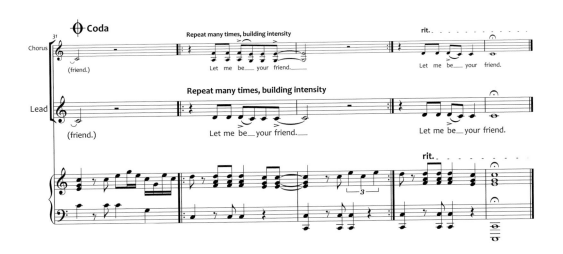

LET'S MAKE A BETTER WORLD

It's common for brothers to fight—not viciously, but they do tussle a lot. One day when my two sons, Robert and Edward, were going at it (again), I thought instead of getting between them, I'd try a different approach. I sat down at the piano and came up with this song on the spot. It really began as a plea to them: can we make a better world in our household? After I sang the first verse, they stopped fighting to listen to the song, so I said to myself, *Wow, this song has possibilities.* What else could I add? "Let's Make a Better World" grew from there.

When I decided I wanted to record the song, I took it to the students at the DeBerry School, where I was the chorus director at the time, to create some words. They added the verse that begins, "I know there's something wrong, / But still I must be strong." A class of teenagers added lyrics about the struggles in their communities, which are revealed in the words, "Can't wait too long, my friend. / If hope is gone, this world is gonna end."

When introducing this song, teachers and chorus leaders can ask, "How can we make a better world in our community? What do you think needs to happen to make a better world? What are the important issues for you? Violence? Incarceration? Lack of jobs? Pollution? Bullying? Racism? Inequality? Injustice?" If they want to, classes can change the words to reflect what they think would make a better world.

 Episode 4: *"Music and Education"*

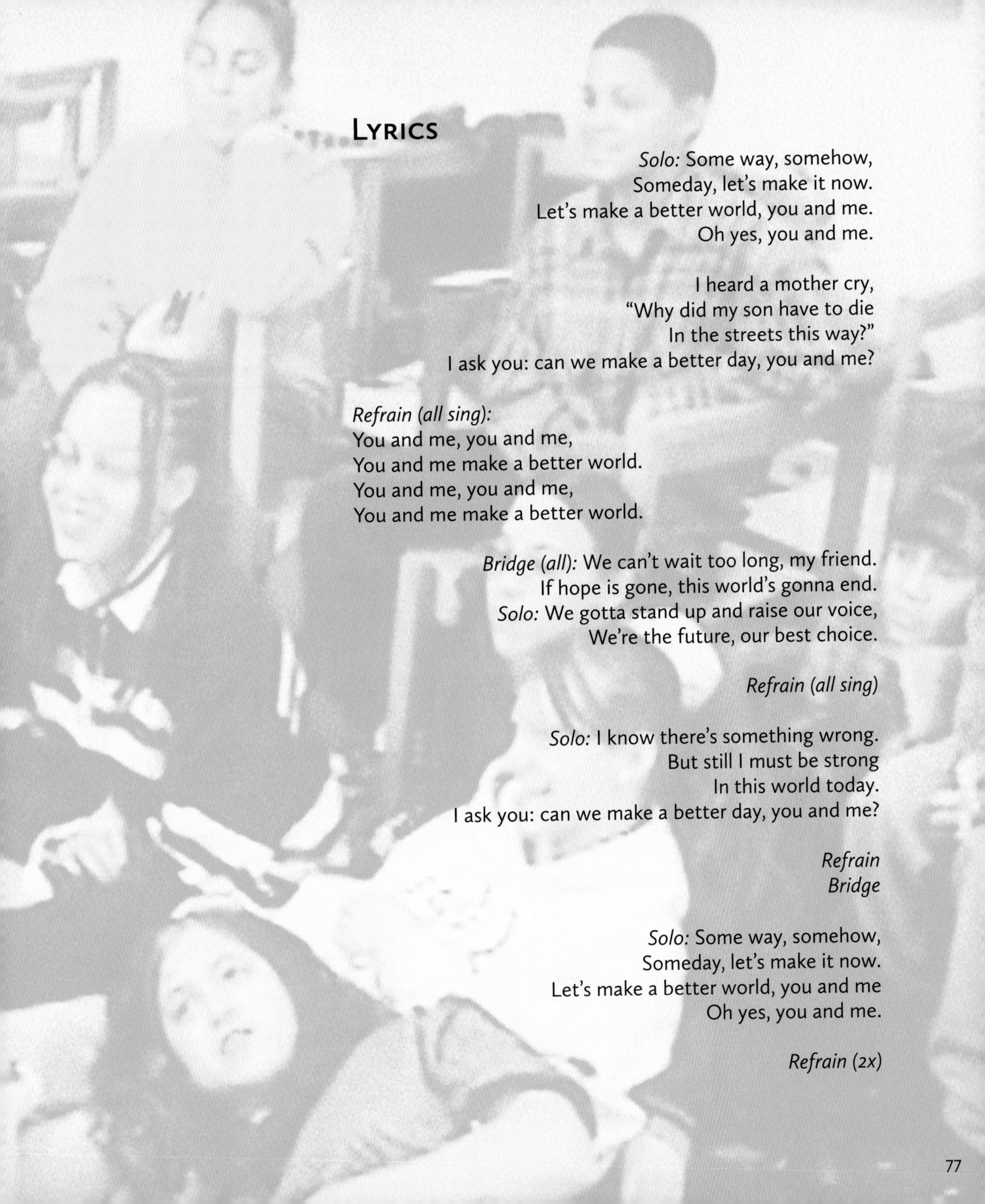

Lyrics

Solo: Some way, somehow,
Someday, let's make it now.
Let's make a better world, you and me.
Oh yes, you and me.

I heard a mother cry,
"Why did my son have to die
In the streets this way?"
I ask you: can we make a better day, you and me?

Refrain (all sing):
You and me, you and me,
You and me make a better world.
You and me, you and me,
You and me make a better world.

Bridge (all): We can't wait too long, my friend.
If hope is gone, this world's gonna end.
Solo: We gotta stand up and raise our voice,
We're the future, our best choice.

Refrain (all sing)

Solo: I know there's something wrong.
But still I must be strong
In this world today.
I ask you: can we make a better day, you and me?

Refrain
Bridge

Solo: Some way, somehow,
Someday, let's make it now.
Let's make a better world, you and me
Oh yes, you and me.

Refrain (2x)

Let's Make a Better World

Jane Sapp

MOVIN' ON

From the time of the Civil War, 85 percent of the population of Greene County, Alabama, was African American, but until the early 1970s, all the local elected officials were white. Prior to the Voting Rights Act of 1965, Black people were denied the right to vote. Of course, after the Voting Rights Act was passed, the African American community sought to have candidates on the ballot that represented their interests as well. However, the Democratic Party of Alabama refused to recognize these new candidates as legitimate because of their race. The African American community responded to this by creating their own party, the National Democratic Party of Alabama, through which African American candidates ran for office. When candidates from the National Democratic Party of Alabama were elected in Greene County, incumbent civil servants filed a series of lawsuits against them. These lawsuits eventually went all the way up to the U.S. Supreme Court. The whole process took about two years, but eventually the court decided in favor of the newly elected African American officials.

We arrived in Greene County after the election of the first African American officials. What inspired me about living in Greene County was the heightened awareness and political involvement of the community. Today the Greene County African American community continues to struggle and organize for full inclusion and democratic participation in the governance of their county and state.

When I wrote this song, I wanted to capture the spirit of progress that permeated Greene County and the feeling of "no matter what, or who, we're gonna keep on movin' on." It's a motivating song that encourages people to jump into the struggle together. Its message is all about not giving up, no matter what you may be struggling with—grades, math, home, or finding a job. I have found that the compelling message of "Movin' On" appeals in many corners and layers of the musical community: high school choruses, community choirs, college and university choruses, and people who want to raise their voices in song for social justice.

Episode 2: *"Resilience and Transformation"*

LYRICS

Solo:
Movin', movin' on. (3x)
Nothing can stop me now,
Nothing can hold me down,
No one can keep me back, 'cause we're

All:
Movin', movin' on. (2x)

Refrain:
Nothing can stop me now,
Nothing can hold me down,
No one can keep me back, 'cause we're
Movin', movin' on. (2x)

Solo:
The road may be rough, the way may be long.
But you got to keep on keepin' on!

Refrain

Solo:
Get your ticket, climb aboard!
This train is headed for a better world!

Refrain

Solo:
Clap your hands, turn around,
Quiet voices are crying out loud!

Refrain

Solo:
Let's work together.
I don't care how long it takes.
We've come this way before and we're

All:
Movin', movin' on. (4x)

Movin' On

Jane Sapp

OLD MACDONALD

This version of "Old MacDonald" is a reworking of the traditional children's song and nursery rhyme. I created a new melody and a new rhythm to give it more energy and to create a more soulful experience of the song. It is flavored with the syncopated rhythms of the African American musical tradition because I didn't want to sing the regular "Old MacDonald had a farm."

I use this story to discuss how each culture brings a unique spice to the table. With this in mind, new cultures can be embraced for their own "special spice," and not feared as something weird and different.

To get young people more involved with this syncopated version, try having them clap and move while singing the song.

 Episode 4: "Music and Education"

LYRICS

Old MacDonald had a farm,
e-i-e-i e-i-o.
And on that farm, he had some ducks,
e-i-e-i e-i-o.
With a "quack, quack" here,
And a quack, quack" there,
Here a "quack," there a "quack,"
everywhere a "quack, quack."
Old MacDonald had a farm,
e-i-e-i e-i-o. Yeah!

Old MacDonald had a farm,
e-i-e-i e-i-o.
And on that farm, he had some sheep,
e-i-e-i e-i-o.
With a "baa, baa" here,
And a "baa, baa" there,
Here a "baa," there a "baa,"
everywhere a "baa, baa."
Old MacDonald had a farm,
e-i-e-i e-i-o. Yeah!

Old MacDonald had a farm,
e-i-e-i e-i-o.
And on that farm, he had some cows,
e-i-e-i e-i-o.
With a "moo, moo" here,
And a "moo, moo" there,
Here a "moo," there a "moo,"
everywhere a "moo, moo."
Old MacDonald had a farm,
e-i-e-i e-i-o. Yeah!

Old MacDonald

Jane Sapp

ONE NOTE WON'T MAKE HARMONY

"One Note Won't Make Harmony" was created in a workshop I led at a high school in Connecticut. I was invited to lead workshops on diversity. My first class was with a group of students who sang in the chorus and who said they were tired of talking or singing about diversity. I said, "Okay, that's fine. What would you like to sing about?" Since they were all members of the chorus, I suggested they tell me what was special about that experience. When they talked, the shape of the song came quickly. The students were so excited about the song that they wanted the next class to hear what they had done. All week, classes added more verses. At the concluding concert at the end of the week, "One Note Won't Make Harmony" was the one song they wanted me to be sure to sing.

The irony of it all was that, though the young people in the chorus in Connecticut didn't want to talk about diversity, creating a song about their chorus led them to make a powerful statement about it: "Every person is a piece of the puzzle, / Everyone is complete together / Every note is a part of the chord, / And one note won't make harmony." Voices of Today, the group I founded in Springfield, Massachusetts, eventually finished the song. I have taught this song to college choruses as well as high school students.

This song has the potential to be used as a lead-in to conversations about the value in each person and the idea that when one person alone tries to dominate the agenda, it stifles the voices and creativity of the group, thereby cheating us all out of a full and rich experience of living together. Teachers and chorus leaders who are working with students on social justice issues can use this song to great effect.

 Episode 7: *"Building Community"*

LYRICS

Every person is a piece of the puzzle,
Everyone is complete together.
Every note is a part of the chord,
And that's what harmony is for

Take different people and put them together,
You'll find strength, wisdom, and beauty.
Open your heart, and share it with me,
'Cause one note won't make harmony.

Everybody together is special,
Everyone adds to our world.
Can't have a puzzle with just one piece,
One note won't make harmony.

Refrain (Solo):
So everyone, let's get together.
There is no need to be alone.
Let's get together to complete the puzzle,
'Cause one note won't make harmony.

The world belongs to everyone,
Those that crawl, walk, or run.
Take care of all living things,
And you will take care of your dreams.

Refrain (Solo)

Every person is a piece of the puzzle,
Everyone is complete together.
Every note is a part of the chord,
And one note won't make,
One note won't make,
And one note won't make harmony.

One Note Won't Make Harmony

Jane Sapp

share it with me,___ 'cause one note won't make___ har-mo - ny.
___ just one piece,   One note won't make___ har-mo - ny.
- ing things,   and you will take care___ of your dreams.

So eve-ry-one, let's get   to - ge - ther.   There is no need to be   a - lone.___   Let's get to-ge-ther to com-

plete   the puz - zle,   'cause one note won't make   har - mo - ny___

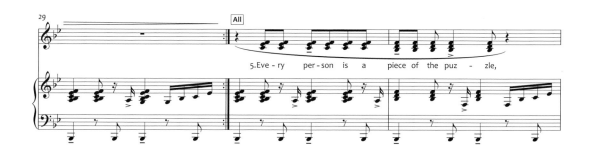

5.Eve - ry per-son is a   piece of the puz - zle,

Eve-ry - one is com plete___ to - ge - ther.___ Eve-ry note is a part of the chord, and one note won't make,___

One note won't make,___ and one note won't make___ har-mo - ny.

RAIN DRIP DROP

This song came out of a workshop I did with schoolchildren in Grand Rapids, Michigan, over the course of five days during their winter break. The group of kids was very diverse, representing a range of demographics and neighborhoods in the area, so it included kids who were not normally in school together. I could tell that there was something special about this group, so I immediately asked them what they wanted to sing about—"What do you want to say?" With no restrictions on their imaginations, the kids really went for it, and one particular student created these lyrics about the sound of the rain. I wrote the music to sound like raindrops to not only accompany the theme of the lyrics but also to show my support for the group's creativity and enthusiasm for their efforts.

A similar approach can also be used when a group or members of a group are resistant to participating in musical exercises like this. I remember another workshop I did where there was a group of boys who just refused to sing, so I said to them, "You're not singing, and that's okay, but you have to do something." I asked them, "What do you wish you were doing?"

They said, "We wish we were playing in the science lab."

So I asked them, "What does it sound like in the lab?"

"Gloopity gloppity!" they said, imitating the sound of liquids being combined in an experiment, so I went ahead and made a song out of "gloopity gloppity," which they loved. In these kinds of situations, when facing resistance from young people in the group, I follow what energizes them. When a song emerges from where they want to go, they will love it.

Episode 4: *"Music and Education"*

Rain Drip Drop

Jane Sapp
with lyrics by Jillian Schultz

LYRICS

Lyrics by Jillian Schultz, age seven,
Grand Rapids, Michigan
Music by Jane Sapp

Rain drip drop rain rain drip drop rain,
Pitter patter, pitter patter, rain, drip!
Drop drip drop rain rain pitter patter,
Drip, drop, rain, rain, rain.

(2x)

SOMEONE SANG FOR ME

"Someone Sang for Me" is another song written by Rose Sanders that I have arranged. Her original version is about voting rights and especially remembering why we vote. Rose composed the song to honor the struggles and sacrifices of our elders who fought for that precious right. The line "Someone suffered and died for me"—I take that literally. The singing, praying, and marching of the Civil Rights movement were often met with violent opposition. For that reason, we must treasure our elders and the legacy of courage and commitment they left us.

I adapted the song to emphasize remembering those whose shoulders we stand on— the courage, faith, struggles, and sacrifices of those who came before us without even knowing who we are, without even knowing our names. Their choices inspire us to think about the generations that will follow us and our responsibility to leave the world better than we found it.

Teachers can use this song as a basis for students to share stories of their ancestors' acts of courage and examples of resilience. Such an exercise can encourage students to empower themselves through their pride and the history of struggle in their own heritage but also to recognize and appreciate the histories of struggle in different communities.

The photograph on page 103 was taken circa 2003 in the Selma, Alabama, Memorial Park, at the annual commemoration of the crossing of Edmund Pettus Bridge, a turning point in the struggle for Voting Rights. The first African American sheriff ever elected in Greene County, Alabama, Sheriff Gilmore, holds the microphone; among those who accompany him in song are Rose Sanders, to his right, and members of the SNCC Freedom Singers.

 Episode 3: *"Freedom and Justice"*

Lyrics

Music and lyrics by Rose Sanders
Arranged by Jane Sapp

Refrain:
(2x; first time, lead only;
second time, all sing)

Someone sang for me.
Someone prayed for me.
Someone marched for me.
Someone suffered and died for me.
And they didn't even know me,
They didn't even know me,
They didn't even know me.

Lead: So we must remember
All: How they lived for us

Lead: And carry their voices with us
All: Wherever we may go

Lead: So we must remember
All: How they lived, how they walked,
how they talked,
How they sacrificed for us.

Refrain
Repeat call-and-response
Refrain

Someone Sang for Me

Rose Sanders
arr. Jane Sapp

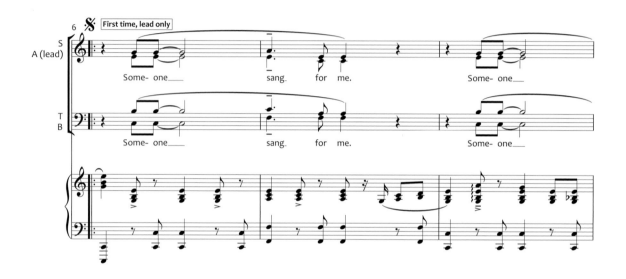

Some one suf-fered and died for me. And they did-n't e - ven know me, they did-n't e - ven know me, they

Some one suf-fered and died_ for me. And they did-n't e - ven know me, they did-n't e - ven know me, they

did-n't e - ven know_____ me.

did-n't e - ven know_____ me.

So we must_____ re-

mem - ber how they lived for us, and car - ry_____ their voi - ces

with us wher-ev-er we may go. So we must_____ re-mem-ber_____

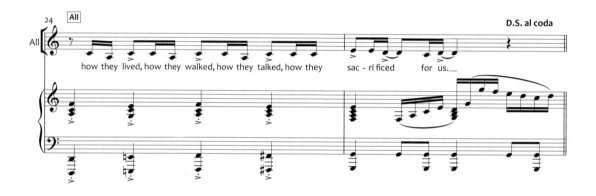

D.S. al coda

how they lived, how they walked, how they talked, how they sac-ri-ficed for us._____

Coda

rit. -

did-n't e - ven know_____ me.

did-n't e - ven know_____ me.

THERE'S A RIVER FLOWING
IN MY SOUL

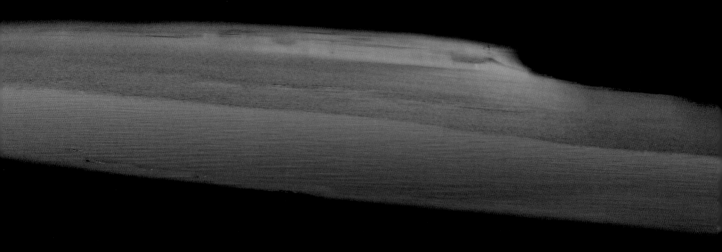

"There's a River Flowing in My Soul" was written in the early 1990s. Rose Sanders was working on the issue of tracking in schools, which she and many others saw as a mechanism to deny advancement opportunities to African American youth. Rose was inspired to write this song to push back against a system that wanted us, and still wants us, to perceive African American schoolchildren as inferior.

The image of a river—something expansive, deep, and ever-flowing, with power and possibilities that go beyond the surface of what can be seen—can be found across many different art forms, including spirituals like "Old Ship of Zion" and poetry like "The Negro Speaks of Rivers" by Langston Hughes.

"There's a River Flowing in My Soul" speaks to something deep inside people, across all ages, races, and backgrounds, because we all have a fundamental need to feel like we are somebody and we matter. This can be applied to individuals as well as communities, as it invites us all to imagine a different, better future where there is equality and everyone is heard and respected. The words are clear, deep, and true. There's plenty of room for everyone to bring themselves to the song. Every struggle and every triumph is at home in this song.

 Episode 3: *"Freedom and Justice"*

LYRICS

Music and lyrics by Rose Sanders   Arranged by Jane Sapp

Lead:
There's a river flowing in my soul. (2x)
And it's telling me that I'm somebody.
There's a river flowing in my soul.

All:
There's a river flowing in my soul. (2x)
And it's telling me that I'm somebody.
There's a river flowing in my soul.

There's a river flowing in my heart. (2x)
And it's telling me that I'm somebody.
There's a river flowing in my heart.

There's a river flowing in my mind. (2x)
And it's telling me that I'm somebody.
There's a river flowing in my mind.

There's a river flowing in my soul. (2x)
And it's telling me that I'm somebody.
There's a river flowing, (2x)
There's a river flowing in my soul.

There's a River Flowing in My Soul

Rose Sanders
arr. Jane Sapp

THIS LITTLE LIGHT OF MINE

One of the best-known African American spirituals, "This Little Light of Mine" has cast its light onto many troubled times. It was often sung during the Civil Rights movement; it was a favorite of Fannie Lou Hamer. This song has offered change and hope. It works just as well as an expression of personal strength, no matter the circumstances. It is sung to lift spirits and to declare, "I have a spirit glowing inside me that's special, and I can feel it." Knowing that I have this warehouse of possibilities within me is a source of joy, hope, and resilience.

I like to sing "This Little Light of Mine" at the beginning of concerts in a way that compels the audience to hear the song for the profound message that it delivers. It's very powerful for audiences to recognize the spirit within them, and even more so for them to recognize it together as a community.

"This Little Light of Mine" is not a singsongy children's tune, but a profound statement that will empower young people and everyone listening to think about what they carry within them and how they let their light shine in the world and with other people. That's why I begin by singing it slow, to make the words clear and to encourage audiences to consider what they are projecting about themselves. Is it life, possibilities, hope? Or something mean and ugly? What is the spirit that lives within you that you want to project?

The black dots and lines on a page of music have no spirit in and of themselves. So when I teach a song, and when I share a song, I focus first on the spirit and the meaning of the words. When you sing, every word is precious. Don't slight any word or the spirit of any word. It is the music and spirit within you that can bring the song to life. Every single word matters, because it's about your voice clearing a path for your truth and making connections for yourself and the people you're singing for.

 Episode 1: *"Imagination and Agency"*

LYRICS

Lead sings first verse, and then improvises on the melody in the verses that follow.

Lead: This little light of mine,
I'm gonna let it shine.
(3x)
Let it shine, let it shine, let it shine.

All: This little light of mine,
I'm gonna let it shine.
(3x)
Let it shine, let it shine, let it shine.

Everywhere I go . . .
All in my room . . .
All over this big wide world . . .
I've got the light of freedom . . .
This little light of mine . . .

This Little Light of Mine

arr. Jane Sapp

I'm gon-na let it shine.___

This lit-tle light of mine,___
Eve-ry - where I go,___
All___ in my room,___
All___ o - ver this big wide world,___
I've got the light of___ free - dom,___
This lit-tle light of mine,___

I'm gon-na let it shine,

___ let it shine,___ let it shine,___ let it shine.

1.2.3.4.5.6.   7.

Slow, with straight eighths

(shine.___)

WE ARE AN AFRICAN PEOPLE

I wrote "We Are an African People" in Birmingham, Alabama, in 1969. It was a time and a place of cultural awakening in the African American community, a period when African Americans were rediscovering and reexamining our histories as well as our cultural, spiritual, and creative roots. These histories had been raised in the past by Marcus Garvey and the Back to Africa movement, but it was in the 1960s and 1970s that we really started talking about and identifying with our connection to Africa. I had been reading about African traditions, cultures, philosophies, and worldviews, and this song arose from my thinking about this research and my own experiences at the time.

The Black Power movement was not just a political movement, but a cultural movement as well. This period was a crossroads in race relations in America and in redefining ourselves as Americans; we were examining our roots in both America and Africa. We were asking: What do those roots represent? What are the strengths they give us? What are our connections to Africa, and what is our inheritance from this connection?

The original intention of this song was to help us realize that there's a place we came from. We didn't suddenly appear in America; Africa is how we got here, through the Middle Passage of the slave trade. It's important to acknowledge that fact and the spiritual and cultural roots of who we are. Written for adult choruses in the Black cultural movement in the 1970s, the original lyrics reinforce this connection and honor Africans as "beautiful people, they're our brothers across the sea." In the accompaniment to the song on my CD, you hear the power of the African drum.

As I taught it to young people in subsequent years, I began to realize that while the song is an expression of the roots of African Americans in the context of our struggle for liberty, it could also be used to express the roots of all of us as immigrants and minorities. We all live on land that originally was home to Native American people. We're either descended from them or from immigrants or from people stolen from their lands. All of us make up the patchwork that is this country. Our struggle for liberty is really an international struggle for justice and equality for all people. This song recognizes both the distinct links between the African continent and the African American community and at the same time reminds us that *Africa is the birthplace of all humanity.*

I wrote this song in 1969, but even today the song still lives whenever and wherever it is taught and sung. It lives in the beauty and pride of our different cultures and communities; it lives in the knowledge of who we are; it lives in the courage of our voices and in our respect for each other. Teachers should tell their students that the "we" is the key of the song—we all make up this patchwork of our country. In the summer of 2015, at the Encampment for Citizenship (a youth leadership program, based that summer in Mississippi), the young people added "We are a gay people," which furthers the evolution of the song and illustrates how it continues to speak to a broad, inclusive audience. This song is always a source of lively discussions, so have at it!

 Episode 2: *"Resilience and Transformation"*

Lyrics

We are an African people, (3x)
Don't you forget it! (2x)

We are a Chippewa people . . .
We are an Asian people . . .
We are a Latino people . . .
We are an Irish people . . .
We are a Hmong people . . .
We are a Jewish people . . .
We are a Muslim people . . .

Bass and Tenor:
We've got to get it together, brother.
Unite ourselves with one another.
We've got to get it together, sister.
Unite ourselves with one another.

Alto:
Stop all these games we play,
Let's make our brighter day today!

Soprano:
We are an African people (2x)

All:
We are an African people (3x)
Don't you forget it! (2x)

We Are an African People

Jane Sapp

We've got to get it to - geth - er, bro - ther. U - nite our - selves with one__ an - oth - er.

We've! U - nite!

Stop all these games__ we play, let's make our bright - er day__ to - day!_

We've got to get it to - geth - er, sis - ter. U - nite our - selves with one__ an - oth - er.

We've! U - nite!

Play at least three times, with new soprano text on each repeat

Repeat as many times as you want!

WE ARE ONE

"We Are One" evolved over several years, with different schools and groups of students each adding ideas from their own experiences. The foundation of the song came from Grand Rapids, Michigan. I asked the students, mostly kids of color, to tell me something wonderful and special about themselves. At first they were playing around and responded by saying things like "I'm beautiful" and "I'm young!" The boys in the class said, "We're strong!"

I responded by kind of teasing them, saying, "You're all that, huh? That makes you perfect?"

This got the kids thinking more, so then they said, "We've still got to grow." One student told me, "My mama said you have to work hard to get anywhere in this world." Another said, "You have to think. You have to use your head more." I took all of these ideas and built the lyrics around them.

Later, when I was working on this song in another city in a workshop with teenage students, the refrain "We are one, we are many" was added. These kids were of an age when they were recognizing themselves and each other as part of a community, which was an important concept to include in a song meant to lift spirits and declare agency.

🎙️ Episode 1: *"Imagination and Agency"*

LYRICS

We are young and beautiful,
Strong and nice,
We can really do something,
Bring our own special spice.
We need to work harder,
This we know,
And we're list'ning and thinking,
And we're ready to grow.

Refrain:
We are one,
We are many.
Together we're strong,
Our voices singing.
And we're list'ning and thinking
And we're ready to grow.
Uh-huh-huh, uh-huh-huh,
Ready to grow.

Hear my voice,
You make a choice,
To respect my pride
And my integrity.
We are who we want to be
Individually,
And we're list'ning and thinking,
And we're ready to grow.

Refrain

We are young and beautiful,
Strong and nice,
We can really do something,
Bring our own special spice.
We need to work harder,
This we know,
And we're list'ning and thinking, (3x)
And we're ready to grow.
Uh-huh-huh, uh-huh-huh,
Ready to grow.

We Are One

Jane Sapp

WE HAVE COME TOO FAR

Some years ago, I served as a cultural facilitator for the Ms. Foundation's annual conference on women and economic development. In this role, I was asked to write a song of resilience that would inspire people, both at the conference and beyond, to continue to struggle for justice—for women and for all those whose lives are diminished by injustices. In thinking about this song, I wanted to remind us all that we have come too far and fought too hard to let anything take us back to where we were before.

The day of the conference arrived and I still had no song. On the way to the conference, on the plane, I knew I had to produce something quickly, and "We Have Come Too Far" emerged. I deliberately wrote it as a round so it would be quick to learn and easy to sing but still maintain the depth of its message. All I had to do was teach the melody and then divide the participants into groups that would go first, second, third, and on and on. I had only heard the song in my mind while I was on the plane, so it was a stunning moment when I heard three hundred voices at the conference singing it together. It's amazing to hear a song like this sung in a round, because as each group comes in with their part, it continues to build in volume and energy, strengthening the ideas the song contains. In subsequent years, young people have changed the line "we can't turn around" to "we won't turn around." I get excited every time I hear it.

In talking with Michael Carter while preparing the podcast that accompanies this book, Michael reminded me that I had written and taught another set of lyrics for this song. It was young Michael and his friends in the chorus at William N. DeBerry Elementary School who drew these lyrics out of me—"We are the children: / Hear our call!/ See me! Hear me! Love me! / Please don't let me fall." I was reflecting on how wonderful, sincere, and creative they all were. I thought to myself, *If people could really see them, hear them, and appreciate and support the treasures they are, their possibilities would be limitless.*

 Episode 2: *"Resilience and Transformation"*

We Have Come Too Far

Jane Sapp

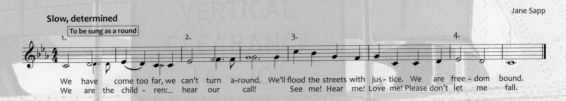

Slow, determined

To be sung as a round

We have come too far, we can't turn a-round. We'll flood the streets with jus-tice. We are free-dom bound.
We are the child-ren:___ hear our call! See me! Hear me! Love me! Please don't let me fall.

LYRICS

To be sung as a round
We have come too far,
We can't turn around.
We'll flood the streets with justice.
We are freedom bound.

For children:
We are the children:
Hear our call!
See me! Hear me! Love me!
Please don't let me fall!

WELCOME TO MY WORLD

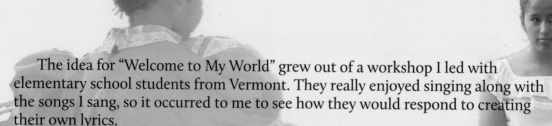

The idea for "Welcome to My World" grew out of a workshop I led with elementary school students from Vermont. They really enjoyed singing along with the songs I sang, so it occurred to me to see how they would respond to creating their own lyrics.

To help the students create the lyrics for this song, I closed my eyes and asked them to describe their community to me, since I did not know it and had never lived there. I asked them prompting questions such as, Where do you live? What does it look like? What are the sights and smells? How would I feel if I spent time in your community? What are the colors in your community? As I kept my eyes closed, one by one the children gently took my hand and whispered to me as if they were sharing their precious secrets. I can still feel the tenderness of those moments. I received the images they shared as a sacred trust and tried to honor them with the music I wrote.

I continued to share this song in other workshops around the country, collecting more lyrics and experiencing more communities through the senses and the imagination of young people.

While most of the lyrics to "Welcome to My World" are quite upbeat, there are some communities where day-to-day life has more challenges, and you have to dig a bit to get them to see another side of their experiences. Such was the case with some young people who described red as the color of blood on the street and the sounds they mentioned were ambulances and police cars. Eventually they drew on other experiences like the smell of hot pies cooking and pizza and strawberries. These words were more in keeping with the spirit of the song. Nevertheless, we continued the conversation about their experiences, and subsequent songs were created to reflect those realities.

 Episode 6: *"We've All Got Stories"*

LYRICS

Refrain:
Welcome to my world!
Please sit and listen to me.
Listen to my story,
It's about you and me.
Oh yeah, it's about you and me.

It's a world of colors.
Green is for the grass that grows.
Brown is for the color of the dirt.
Black is for my people.
Oh yeah, black is for my people.

Refrain

Red is for the color of my house.
Purple's for the mountains.
Blue is for the sky so bright.
White is for the snowflakes falling.
Oh yeah, white is for the snow-
flakes falling.

Refrain

I can smell the green, green grass,
And the fresh air all around,
Pizza, and strawberries.
Smell the hot pies cooking.
Oh yeah, smell the hot pies cooking.

Refrain

Can't you hear the dogs barking,
Babies crying, people singing?
I can hear the horns beeping,
Kids laughing everywhere
Oh yeah, kids laughing everywhere.

Refrain

Welcome to My World

Jane Sapp

Brown is for the co - lor of the dirt. Black is for my peo - ple. Oh__ yeah,
Blue is for the sky so bright.__ White is for the snow-flakes fall - ing. Oh__ yeah,
piz - za, and straw - ber - ries.__ Smell the hot pies cook - ing. Oh__ yeah,
I can hear the horns__ beep - ing, Kids laugh-ing ev - ery- where.__ Oh__ yeah,

black is for my peo - ple.
white is for the snow-flakes fall - ing.
smell the hot pies cook - ing.
kids laugh-ing ev - ery - where.__

it's a - bout you and__ me.

Oh yeah,__ it's a - bout you and__ me.__

rit.

WE'VE ALL GOT STORIES

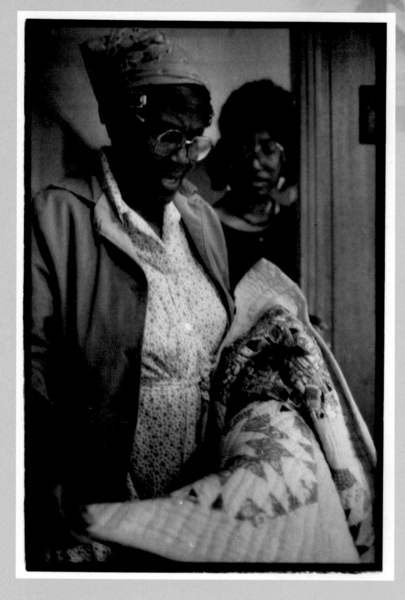

Episode 6: *"We've All Got Stories"*

"We've All Got Stories" is another song for which students created lyrics. Its strength lies in the affirmation that children's knowledge is valuable and worth contributing. I often tell young people, "Nobody knows everything, but everybody knows something. So tell me the special things that you know." This song encourages young people to share with each other and to understand that we all have unique experiences.

This allows students to hear stories about a variety of experiences that other children in other parts of the country have. For some it may be the first time they've considered the possibility that children live differently in different parts of the world. For instance: "This is what kids in Alabama said—'In the winter, I wear shoes with no socks.' Can you imagine this in Vermont?"

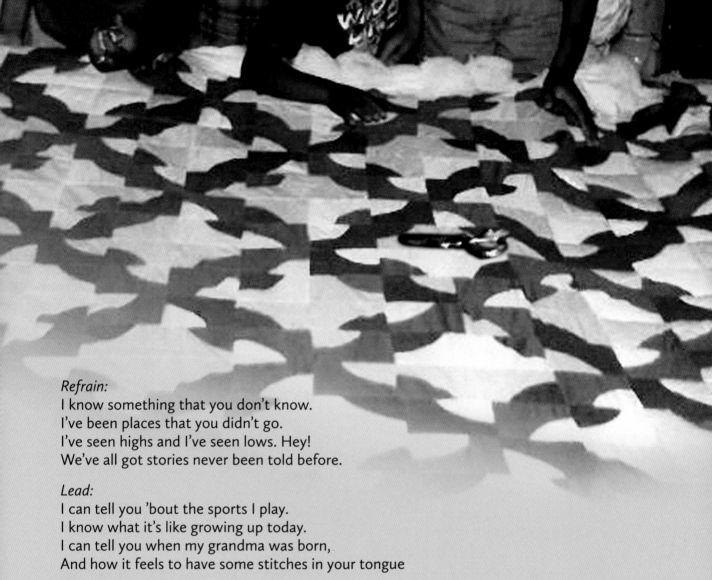

Refrain:
I know something that you don't know.
I've been places that you didn't go.
I've seen highs and I've seen lows. Hey!
We've all got stories never been told before.

Lead:
I can tell you 'bout the sports I play.
I know what it's like growing up today.
I can tell you when my grandma was born,
And how it feels to have some stitches in your tongue

Refrain

Lead:
I can tell you why the moon shines bright.
I have seen the stars fall down at night.
I can still have fun even when it's hot. Hot!
And in the winter, I wear shoes with no socks.

Refrain

We've all got stories, (2x)
We've all got stories never been told before.

We've All Got Stories

Jane Sapp

WITHOUT FREEDOM

"Without Freedom" was written with a fifth-grade class at Wheeler Elementary School in Burlington, Vermont, around the time of Martin Luther King Jr. Day. This class included Black, white, and Vietnamese kids. As I usually do, I asked the kids what they wanted to talk about and told them that what they said would become a song. I went to the blackboard to write the topics they suggested.

The suggestions from the kids ranged from the sublime to the totally ridiculous: "My dog!" "My cat!" "My baby brother!" "How about the boogers in your nose?!" But one student said, "How about freedom?"

I then told the class they would vote to choose which of these ideas to make into a song. To my surprise, freedom won. Freedom was the only abstract idea on the list, but it was one that obviously resonated in their young lives.

So I asked, "What does freedom mean to you? What are you doing when you're feeling free? What is it like if you don't have freedom?"

They said things like "You'll be sad" and "You'll cry." One student even said, "You'll be a slave," and I kept that in mind. Then the class started to get serious: "If you don't have it, a lot of people will die"; "Without freedom, there may be no today." In the middle of all of this, I asked them what they would be doing if they felt *really* free. A group of Vietnamese students was sitting together in a corner, and when they finally spoke, they said, "Popping firecrackers off the ground!" Now, how could I incorporate that alongside everything else?

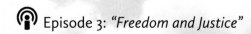 Episode 3: *"Freedom and Justice"*

When I played the finished song for the class the next day, I could see the kids' eyes light up when they recognized their individual contributions, especially the firecrackers kids. This was a part of their tradition and something they didn't feel free to do there in Burlington at that time.

When teaching this song or any song to students, try to talk about what's inside the song: What is its meaning? What is it trying to say? What is its spirit? What does it make you think about? Every songwriter is trying to say something, and every listener hears the song differently. The important thing is to go exploring for meaning. This is a way to have conversations with young people about what they're thinking. For instance, when I play this song for other classes, I tell them, "This is what a class from Burlington said when they were talking about freedom." Then I ask, "What does it mean to you? What would you say?" That gives agency to young people so they can begin to discover that what they think matters and that their voices have value and deserve to be heard. Giving shape and form to their thoughts through song strengthens their image of themselves as reflective and creative young people. It's a transformative experience when young people realize, "Wow, I wrote a song and it sounds like *that*." When the fifth grade class at Wheeler Elementary heard their song, "Without Freedom," they weren't hearing it just inside their heads but in their hearts too. What we and they hear is them giving birth to their own intelligence, dignity, and spirit.

LYRICS

Without freedom, lots of people die.
Without freedom, you could be a slave.
Without freedom, there may be no today,
Without freedom, without freedom.

Freedom is all around you,
You can feel it coming from your heart.
You can make choices for yourself.
It's a place where you can make a start.

Freedom is coming tomorrow,
No one can beat you or boss you around.
It's spreading all over the big wide world
Like firecrackers poppin' off the ground.

Without freedom, lots of people die.
Without freedom, you could be a slave.
Without freedom, there may be no today,
Without freedom, without freedom.

Without Freedom

Jane Sapp

LET'S MAKE A BETTER WORLD PODCAST

Conversations about cultural work with Jane Sapp and Cynthia (Cindy) Cohen
Introduced by Michael Carter
Produced by David Briand
Available online at janesapp.org

All the songs in the songbook can be heard on the podcast that accompanies the book. These renditions illustrate one way the songs can be interpreted, but we encourage people to be creative. Improvise! Add new verses! Make the songs work in your classroom and for your chorus!

Episode 1: Imagination and Agency
Songs:
This Little Light of Mine
I Want to Be Strong
We Are One
If I Had the World in My Hands

Episode 2: Resilience and Transformation
Guest: Michael Carter,
music educator and cultural worker
Songs:
We Are an African People
We Have Come Too Far
Movin' On
I Want to Lift My Sister Up

Episode 3: Freedom and Justice
Guest: Rose Sanders,
civil rights lawyer, activist, cultural worker, and
composer
Songs:
Someone Sang for Me
Without Freedom
There's a River Flowing in My Soul

Episode 4: Music and Education
Guest: Sandra Nicolucci, music educator
Songs:
I Want to Know
Everybody Makes a Difference
Let's Make a Better World
I Feel Music Everywhere
Old MacDonald
Rain Drip Drop
Did You Hear That?

Episode 5: Music and Human Rights
Guest: Suzanne Pharr,
feminist, antiracist, and LGBTQ activist and author
Songs:
If You Miss Me from the Back of the Bus
Ain't You Got a Right

Episode 6: We've All Got Stories
Guest: LaShawn Simmons,
poet, cultural activist, and Brandeis alumna
Songs:
We've All Got Stories
Welcome to My World
Dream, Dream

Episode 7: Building Community
Songs:
I Want to Be Strong
One Note Won't Make Harmony
Let Me Be Your Friend